WHEN THE
PAST AND THE
PRESENT

COLLIDE

THE FUTURE
IS CHANGED

KELLY MCINTIRE

Edited and ebook design by Kristen Corrects, Inc.
Cover art design by Victoria Wolf, Red Wolf Marketing
Book formatting by Andrea Constantine

First edition published 2019

Time Twisted is dedicated to Margaret and Harold Webster and Barbara and Wendell McIntire, known to their grandchildren as Mimi and Biggie and Nanny and Papa – timeless examples of wonderful grandparents.

CHAPTER ONE

The sun was bright in the clear blue sky and a breeze softened the August heat. It was a perfect Saturday morning in Cabot Corner, Iowa, and thirteen year-old Lea Grant spent it mucking the stalls in the horse barn on her family's farm. There were many dull chores to do on a farm, but caring for the horses wasn't one of them. She liked the way they nuzzled her shoulder and softly whinnied when she brushed their manes. Lea was good to all of the horses, but she always gave her horse Starburst a little extra attention.

"Sorry, Starburst, not today," Lea said, rubbing the horse's long nose. They would usually go for a ride when she was done caring for her, but today Lea had to sit with her grandmother, so there wasn't time. Lea was never happy about babysitting Gramma, and on a beautiful summer Saturday, she dreaded it even more.

Sighing, Lea checked her phone. She was running late! Reluctantly, she put Starburst's brush away and gave her one more pat. She closed the stall a little more forcefully than necessary, and muttered something her mother wouldn't approve of under her breath as she left the barn and started up the hill to the house. Gramma wasn't nearly as good company as the horses.

Lea lunged up the hill, her breath coming in short bursts. Gramma Perkins had come to live with Lea's family just over a year ago. Although Gramma had lived in Cabot Corner most of her life, she left town twelve years ago after Grampa Perkins died and went to live with her brother, Great Uncle Carlton, in a small town in Virginia. They had always been close, and Gramma wanted to escape the cold Iowa winters. Lea was just a baby when Gramma moved. Even though Gramma came back frequently to visit, it wasn't enough.

I don't even really know her, Lea thought bitterly.

Besides, it wasn't like Lea had a chance to know Gramma now. Gramma had Alzheimer's disease, and although she could remember almost everything from when she was much younger, Gramma remembered very little from the present. Sometimes she didn't even know who Lea was.

Uncle Carlton couldn't take care of her, so Gramma came to live with Lea's family.

Alzheimer's was a strange illness. Gramma's body seemed healthy enough, but her brain was sick, which caused her to be confused and made her behave strangely. Just a few weeks ago she had insisted on wearing a winter coat, a hat, and gloves to sit outside even though it was eighty-three degrees. For some reason, she thought it was Christmas Day back in the 1940s and she was getting ready to go to her grandmother's house for dinner. She was even singing Christmas carols!

Alzheimer's disease also made Gramma do things that were dangerous. One night when she still lived in Virginia, she got out of bed and walked out of the house, still in her nightgown. Uncle Carlton didn't even know she was gone until the next morning. It took the police almost all day to locate Gramma. They finally found her wandering through wooded trails in a park near her home. It was after that when Lea's parents decided to have Gramma move to the farm.

Lea reached the crest of the hill and breathed. It was probably best for Gramma to move in with the family, but she wasn't so sure it was good *for* the family. Gramma was a lot of work. She couldn't stay home alone, and Lea's mother had to make sure Gramma ate and got dressed. *Gramma even needs to be reminded to use the bathroom*, Lea thought, grimacing. A nurse came in a few times a week to help her shower, and sometimes volunteers from the church would come by and read to her, but most of Gramma's care fell on Lea's mom.

And, of course…more work for us.

Lea knew it was selfish, but she resented that she had to spend more time helping her younger siblings because her mom couldn't. Lea didn't have to do much for Sam, her eleven-year-old-brother, except sometimes help him with his homework, but she was expected to help out with the twins, Michael and Emily. They were only six, so they needed to be watched almost as much as Gramma did.

But deep down, Lea wondered if the problem she had with Gramma was the problem Gramma seemed to have with *her*. Gramma was nice to Sam—actually, she thought he was her brother, Carlton, who Sam looked like when Carlton was a teenager. Since Gramma lived mostly in the past, she was very comfortable with him. Lea and Gramma didn't get along. Gramma didn't like the way Lea dressed— she thought Lea's shorts were too short, and that tank tops were inappropriate, even on the hottest days of summer. Gramma loved chocolate and always had a dish of it next to her chair. She was happy to share with Carlton and the twins, but if Lea ever dared to take a piece, Gramma would yell, "That chocolate is for me. Don't you touch it!" Lea wasn't sure if this made her sad or angry, but no matter what, she didn't like spending time with Gramma.

Gramma was sitting on the back screen porch when Lea got to the house. She stared out blankly at the cornfield, mumbling something. As Lea sat down, she realized that Gramma was reciting lines from a play.

"Hi Gramma, what are you doing?"

Gramma ignored Lea and went on with her lines.

Her grandmother had always had a role in her high school plays, Lea knew. It was a big part of her life when she was younger. Besides Grampa, theater had been the great love of Gramma's life.

So Gramma can't remember what she ate for breakfast, but she can remember every line from a play she was in almost sixty years ago?

Gramma went on with a few more lines then stopped rather abruptly. Her gaze shifted to Lea. "Those shorts are too short."

Lea pushed down a wave of anger and disappointment, pressing her lips together to keep from saying something she shouldn't. Gramma just turned her head back toward the field.

She gazed at Gramma, wishing that she and Gramma had the kind of relationship that her friend Nicole had with her grandmother. Nicole's Nana made cookies for Nicole and her sisters, and even took them on outings. Best of all, she told them stories about when she was a girl. Lea loved hearing her tales—it was just like traveling back in time.

Even though Gramma thought she was living in the 1950s, she couldn't tell her stories because of Alzheimer's. And even on the days when Gramma could talk a little about her childhood, she didn't seem to want Lea around long enough to tell her.

Lea sighed. Would she ever connect with her grand-mother?

CHAPTER TWO

S undays on the Grant Farm meant church followed by a big country breakfast. Before Gramma came to live with them, everyone in the family went to church together. But now, someone had to stay home and watch her. At first, they tried to bring Gramma to church with them, but after she stood up in the middle of the service and loudly accused the organist of stealing money from the offering plate, Lea's mom decided that Gramma would no longer attend. Today it was Lea's turn to stay home, which meant two days in a row of watching Gramma.

The rest of the family piled into their old Chevy Suburban, and Lea plunked down in the leather recliner in Gramma's room, where Gramma was sitting in her chair, staring into space. Gramma's room used to be a den next to the kitchen where Lea, Carlton, and the twins played video games and spent time with their friends. Lea missed having a place where the kids could all hang out together. It wasn't so bad in the summer because they could go to the barn or just be outside. But in the winter there was no place to get away from the adults. It didn't seem fair to Lea, but there was no use arguing with her parents about it. She had already tried that and they told her she was being selfish.

Gramma's blank stare abruptly changed to a scowl. "Don't eat my chocolate," she ordered. Lea sighed and tried to change the subject.

"Do you want me to read to you, or do you want to watch TV?"

"I'm going to the movies with Harry," Gramma said, turning her head away from Lea. "I'm waiting for him to pick me up."

Lea stood. "I'll leave you alone for a bit, Gramma," she said.

She went to the porch that was off Gramma's room. When Gramma moved in, Dad installed a door with a lock hidden at the top. Unless Gramma was being carefully watched, the door was always locked. Lea reached up to release the lock and walked onto the porch. She buried herself in her phone, texting a couple of friends and playing a game.

Forty-five minutes later, Lea looked in on Gramma. She was sound asleep. Smiling, Lea went into the kitchen to get some juice and a snack. *Everyone will be home soon and I can do whatever I want!* She would take Starburst for a long ride, to make up for yesterday.

Lea glanced at the clock. Her family should be home any minute. She walked into Gramma's room, careful not to make any noise, but as she looked in, she gasped.

"Gramma?"

Gramma wasn't in her chair.

Lea ran onto the porch. Gramma wasn't there either.

The porch door was wide open, swinging back and forth in the morning breeze.

Oh no.

Panic overwhelmed Lea and she was glued to the floor, unable to move. She had forgotten to lock the door when she came in from the porch. Now Gramma was somewhere outside…and Lea was going to be in a lot of trouble with her parents.

Lea's feet decided to work and she sprang into action. She ran into the back yard, her eyes scanning from the swing set to the gate that opened into the back pasture. There was no sign of Gramma anywhere.

"Gramma? Gramma!"

Lea ran around the side yard to the front of the house, hoping that Gramma would be there, but no luck.

The Suburban came rumbling down the road and up the driveway.

"Gramma's missing," Lea wailed, as her family piled out of the truck. "She fell asleep and I went out on the porch for a few minutes. I came back in to get some juice and when I checked on her again, she was gone. I'm sorry. I didn't think she'd wake up that fast and I was planning on going back to the porch. I know I should have locked the door. I just didn't think…"

There was a moment of stunned silence, then Mom took over.

"We didn't see her on the road. She must still be somewhere on the farm. Lea and Sam, look in the back pastures. Michael and Emily, make sure she isn't somewhere in the house. Dad will take the gator into the cornfield. I'll start calling the neighbors and notify the police."

Lea and Sam ran to the cow pasture, but Gramma was nowhere to be found.

"I can't believe she got out," Lea said, her voice cracking. "I never should have left her alone, but she didn't want me around. She said that Grampa Harry was taking her to the movies. I went to the porch so she could be alone."

"Do you think she's trying to get to the movie theater?" Sam asked. "Maybe when Grampa Harry didn't show she thought she was supposed to meet him there."

Sam and Lea took off toward the house, hoping that Sam was right. Dad was just coming up from the cornfield and stopped the gator so Leah and Sam could jump in. Sam quickly explained what they thought was going on as they drove back to the house.

"I don't know if Gramma knows how to get to the movie theater," Dad said, "but it's worth a try." He parked the gator next to the Suburban and they jumped into the truck. They drove slowly down the road, looking for Gramma on both sides of the street. The road into town was usually very busy, but on a Sunday morning there was less traffic than usual.

The Cabot Corner Cinema 8 was located next to a small strip mall about a mile from the Grant Farm. Dad pulled the truck into the parking lot. It was still too early for the theater to open, so they knew Gramma wasn't inside. They got out and started to look around, but she wasn't in the parking lot or wandering near the strip mall either. Dejected, they got back in the Suburban and headed home.

Where could she be? Lea's stomach twisted with guilt. *What if she gets hurt?*

Mom was in the driveway talking on her phone when they arrived home. She hung up quickly, and ran over to the driver's side window as they came to a stop. "I just got a call from Nancy Smith. She's with Gramma on Main Street. Gramma was wandering up and down the street looking for the movie theater."

"How did she get there?" Lea asked in amazement.

"She must have walked," Mom answered. "They're sitting on a bench across from the church."

"We'll go get her," Dad said, putting the vehicle in reverse.

They drove in silence to Main Street, Lea's mind abuzz. How could Gramma get out while she was watching her? She was so embarrassed, and she was grateful that neither Sam nor Dad were bringing that up.

"There they are!" Dad slowed the Suburban and pointed to Gramma and Nancy Smith sitting on the bench, laughing together. Dad pulled over and Sam jumped out.

"Hi Carlton. I'm waiting for Harry to meet me for a movie," Gramma said with a smile.

Nancy looked a little worried, but Sam knew what to do. "The movie theater isn't opened yet. Let's go have breakfast."

Lea watched as Sam coaxed Gramma into the truck.

"It was nice to see you, Genny," yelled Nancy as Gramma got into the Suburban. "Enjoy your breakfast."

Gramma waved back at Nancy as they drove away.

Gramma was safe—that's all that mattered—but Lea was sad that she and Gramma didn't have a relationship like Gramma and Sam had. *Why does she respond so well to him, but doesn't want anything to do with me?* As tears welled in her eyes, Lea sent off a silent wish that somehow, some way, she and Gramma would learn to get along.

CHAPTER THREE

During the school year, Monday was Lea's least favorite day of the week—but in the summer, it was the day she looked forward to the most. There was far less farm work to do because the hired hands were back from the weekend break, and it was the day the twins went on their weekly field trip with the town recreation department. Once she took care of the horses, Lea had the day to herself. She rode Starburst through the fields and into the woods, stopping at the creek to let her have a drink. After their ride, Lea left Starburst in the pasture with the other horses and she walked up the hill to the house, rubbing the sleep out of her eyes. She hadn't slept much the night before because of everything that had happened with Gramma.

The hammock at the edge of their property near the woods swayed in the breeze, beckoning her. The sky had been clear blue all morning, but now a few fluffy white clouds were rolling in. The wind had picked up slightly, but the sun was still bright. On the hammock, Lea studied the newly formed clouds—one looked like an elephant, another like a fish, and still another like an angel. As the wind blew gently, they moved and changed form, the elephant becoming a blob until it transformed into a boat, the fish and the angel morphing together into something indistinguishable. Lea closed her eyes.

A huge gust of wind swung the hammock almost upside down. She jolted and her eyes flew open. "Hey!" she yelled, expecting to see Sam pushing her. But Sam wasn't there. No one was.

Just as the hammock came back down, another gust of wind swung it in the opposite direction. Lea held on tightly, sure that it was about to dump her on the ground. The hammock hurtled one direction and another, getting more height with each thrust. Lea screamed, trying to hold on. Her grip was loosening with each rotation, until finally the wind won, plucking her out of the hammock and catapulting her into the sky.

She was immersed in a cloud of darkness—flipping, turning, and screaming into what seemed like oblivion.

Then suddenly, the cloud cleared, the turmoil eased, and

Lea floated softly to the ground. The sun had returned.

But Lea was no longer on the farm.

She stood at the side of a busy street, with both cars and foot traffic. Nothing looked normal. In fact, everything seemed outdated. The cars driving by looked like the antique cars that were always on display at the county fair, and the people looked different too. Their clothes and hairstyles were like those the characters wore in the old sitcoms that Mom put on TV for Gramma.

Stunned by her flight and sudden change in location, Lea sat down on a nearby sidewalk bench. *What happened?* She noticed Clark's Hardware, an old-fashioned store with a front porch, to her left, and a general store on her right. A sign in the window of the general store advertised Coca-Cola for five cents a bottle. *What? Soda is $1.50 at the convenience store down the street from the farm.* Across the street, a movie theater with an oversized marquis touted a 7:00 PM showing of *From Here to Eternity*. She had never heard of it. Lea had a queasy feeling in her stomach, and her palms were beginning to sweat. Something weird was going on.

A young girl wearing a long puffy skirt and saddle shoes walked by and gave her a strange look. Then Lea noticed a group of young boys staring at her, giggling and pointing at her. Two older women walked by, and one said to the other, "She should put some clothes on. What would her mother say?"

Denim shorts, a tank top, and flip-flops were what Lea always wore, but apparently it wasn't the style here. All of the women and girls were wearing dresses or skirts, and although the boys were wearing jeans and sneakers, they didn't look like the ones her brother or her friends from school wore.

Experiencing a sudden feeling of self-consciousness, Lea stood from the bench. *Where am I?* She needed to get out of public view. Lea walked into the general store, hoping to grab a Coke with the change in her pocket.

The inside looked very different from the stores she was used to. The floor was made of worn-out wood, and there were only a few lights, making the store seem dark. The food on the shelves had packaging she had never seen before.

A man and a woman stood behind a wooden counter next to a cash register. The smiles of greeting when Lea first walked through the door were quickly replaced with looks of confusion when they got a full look at her.

Lea's eyes fell on an ice chest with an outdated Coca-Cola logo. She opened the chest, grabbed a glass bottle of soda, and walked to the counter to pay. The cash register was interesting. It had raised circular buttons with numbers on them that the woman pressed to make the cash drawer open with a loud *clang*. There wasn't a rubber conveyer belt or a scanner to be found, so Lea put the bottle on the counter and pulled out her change.

"That'll be five cents," the woman said.

Lea handed the woman her money and was surprised when the man picked up her bottle of Coke. He used a bottle opener to take the cap off and he handed it back to Lea.

"Thank you," she said, then started walking to the door.

"Dear, are you okay?" the woman called after her. "Do you need anything?"

"No," Lea answered, "I'm fine," and quickly walked outside.

So now I'm back outside with a Coke and I still have no idea where I am, Lea thought. She should get off Main Street where she was attracting so much attention. She spied an alley next to the hardware store—she would be less conspicuous there. Once alone in the alley, she pulled out her phone to text her friend Nicole. Nicole would know what to do.

But Lea couldn't get her phone to turn on. A feeling of hopelessness washed over her. Where was she? Why was everything so strange?

Feeling very alone, but still not wanting to return to the busy street, Lea walked the rest of the way down the alley to a small park with a fountain and a bench. A girl of about fifteen or sixteen was sitting on the bench, reading a book. She jumped when she saw Lea, as if she was startled. But her surprise turned to curiosity as she looked Lea up and down.

"Hi," she said a little slowly. "Are you okay? You look, um…well, underdressed, or maybe even not dressed. Sorry,

I don't want to insult you, but I'm surprised you were allowed out of the house like that."

"Yes, I'm fine," Lea said, annoyed. "Everyone dresses like this where I'm from."

"Well, you might want to get some new clothes if you plan to stay around here. Your name will be mud in no time if you keep dressing like that."

Lea stared at the girl, dumbfounded, not sure what to say or think. She *was* insulted, but from what she had seen on the main road and in the store, Lea knew the girl was right. But how was she supposed to get new clothes? She didn't even want new clothes. She just wanted to get back to the farm, although she had no idea how to do that. She didn't have any money, or know anyone, and worst of all, she couldn't use her phone.

For the first time in her life, Lea was truly afraid.

Tears welled up in her eyes. Before she could turn away, a few overflowed and fell down her face.

"Well, don't cry," the girl said. "I'm Genevieve."

"I'm Lea." She sniffled back her tears.

"Nice to meet you," Genevieve said politely. And then she added, "You look nervous."

"I'm not," Lea lied. "I'm just new around here and I'm not sure where anything is and I don't know anyone."

"Well, those are all good reasons to be nervous," Genevieve said. "Nothing wrong with being nervous when you're in a place where you don't know anyone. But honestly, you should get some new clothes. No one here dresses like that. If you want to make friends, you should at least try to fit in."

"I don't have any money with me, so these will have to do," Lea answered truthfully. She looked down at her clothes.

Genevieve looked at Lea closely for a minute before speaking, as if she was trying to decide something. "My parents always say that we should help those in need, so I guess I should help you. Would you like to borrow some clothes so you don't have to wear those rags?"

She thinks I'm needy! Lea was embarrassed as she looked down at her shorts. Although shredded denim was popular among her friends, it probably did look a little ragged to Genevieve. And it would probably be easier to figure out a plan if she fit in better.

"Thanks," Lea said reluctantly. "I guess I should."

"Come with me." Genevieve stood from the bench.

Lea followed Genevieve back to the alley and into a side door of the hardware store.

"My parents own the hardware store," Genevieve explained over her shoulder. "We live in the apartment above it."

The girls walked through a back storage space and up a flight of stairs into the kitchen of a large apartment. Lea followed Genevieve across a sitting room and into one of the back bedrooms. Nobody else seemed to be home.

Genevieve closed the door and opened a closet filled with skirts and blouses. Within minutes Lea had traded her shorts, tank top, and flip-flops for a longer-than-she-liked skirt that puffed out at the bottom, a white short-sleeved blouse, and worn-out saddle shoes. Lea gazed at herself in a mirror.

I look ridiculous.

Genevieve gave her a nod of approval. "Much better. You look much more respectable."

"Thanks," Lea mumbled, rather unenthusiastically.

"I hate to be rude, but I have to go," Genevieve said. "I'm supposed to be meeting someone, and now I'm late. But if you want to stop by the hardware store around 4:00, I can show you around town before dinner."

The girls hurried down the stairs and back to the alley. Saying a quick goodbye, Genevieve went back toward the park, and Lea, now dressed more appropriately, returned to the street where she had originally found herself. She walked in front of the hardware store, and then by the general store, then passed a bakery and a small breakfast shop. When she came to a penny candy store, she stopped and entered, hearing the faint *tink* of the bell on the door.

The store had more candy in one place than Lea had ever seen. Instead of being pre-packaged and stacked on a shelf, the different types of candy were in bins, each one with a scoop. Lea looked around. Small brown bags were available to put your selection in, and then each bag was weighed on a scale to determine its price. Lea looked at the prices and was shocked. Why was everything so cheap? She wished she had taken the change from her shorts so she could buy a few pieces of licorice or a candy necklace.

Lea continued her walk, exploring this strange Main Street. The rest of the stores weren't that interesting, but when she came to the post office, Lea stopped in her tracks. The front of the building proudly read *CABOT CORNER, IOWA*. She read the words again, still not trusting what they said. Lea looked up and down and across the street, turning in a circle as she took everything in.

Can this really be Cabot Corner? Lea wondered. *It looks so different.*

But then in the distance she saw Donnelly Park, the site of Fourth of July fireworks and the annual Old Home Day celebration. Then, the Baptist church across the street from the park. The rest of the street was harder to recognize. A grand movie theater took up quite a bit of the street, but it wasn't part of the landscape Lea was familiar with—nor were most of the stores that lined both sides of the street.

Lea walked toward Donnelly Park, still amazed by this unfamiliar version of her hometown, wondering if this was a dream. *Maybe when I fell out of the hammock during the windstorm I hit my head and I'm hallucinating.* She ignored the gut feeling telling her no, that she was most definitely awake. She didn't have a headache or feel disoriented.

She hurried to a newspaper rack in front of the park entrance and looked at the date on the daily paper: *August 17, 1953.* She knew it was August 17—but 1953? How was that possible?

Lea's brain seemed to move at a snail's pace as her mind wrapped around the thought: Could she have traveled back in time? That seemed crazy, but… A strange feeling began to creep into Lea's stomach and her breath stuck in her chest.

I'm in 1953?

Her vision narrowed and her head began to spin.

Everything around her went black.

The next thing Lea knew, she was sitting on the sidewalk in front of the park and a boy of about fourteen was supporting her back.

"Are you okay?" he asked, backing away as Lea sat up straight on her own. "I caught you before you hit your head. You were just sort of swaying back and forth before you fell."

Lea was definitely out of sorts, but there was something familiar about the boy that made her feel comfortable. As her head cleared she realized how much the boy looked like Sam. Lea blinked a few times, just to make sure she wasn't seeing things. Other than his clothes, the boy was a dead-ringer for her brother. Was it possible that Sam had ended up in 1953 too?

"Sam? Are you here too?"

The boy looked confused. "I'm not Sam. Do you need a doctor or should I find your mother?"

"No. I'm okay. I've just had a strange day," Lea said as she stood up. "Thanks for helping me."

Lea walked away quickly, if not a bit wobbly, into Donnelly Park before the boy could ask any more questions. She had no idea what was going on, and she needed some time to figure it all out. She couldn't explain any of it, but somehow she had been transported back to 1953. She let that thought settle into her mind. *I'm in 1953.* Her heartbeat quickened. *And I have no idea how to get home.*

As weird and scary as the situation was, she found her emotions moving toward curiosity. Did this sort of thing happen all the time, but no one ever talked about it when they got back to the year they belonged in? Maybe when you got back, you couldn't remember anything that had happened. Or maybe it wasn't possible to go back. Maybe this is what happened to people who just disappeared— perhaps they just ended up in a different decade or even century. Lea stopped her thoughts. That was too scary to consider right now.

She left Donnelly Park and continued walking up Main Street, away from the hardware store. In 1953, there was a clock in the middle of the sidewalk in front of town hall, and Lea was surprised that it was already nearly 4:00. Did time pass more quickly during time travel? She hurried back toward the hardware store to meet Genevieve.

Genevieve was waiting for Lea on the front porch of the hardware store, chewing on a Twizzler stick. As Lea approached, she held one out to Lea.

"Thanks," Lea said. She hadn't eaten anything since breakfast and was starving.

"Sorry I had to run off before," Genevieve said. "I promised Harold I'd meet him by the fountain. I always meet him there when he's on his way to work."

"Is Harold your boyfriend?"

"Sort of, I guess," answered Genevieve, looking at Lea sideways as they walked down the street. "We've liked each other since we were little, but I wasn't allowed to date until I turned sixteen, and that just happened. We're going to the movies tonight. Other than going to school dances, where there are more adults than kids, it's my first date ever." She grinned, giddy. "I can't wait."

The two girls walked down Main Street, passing the town library, which Lea realized had been renovated since 1953, and a Laundromat, which no longer existed in Lea's time. A little farther down the street was a drug store that looked nothing like the CVS and Walgreens that Lea was familiar with. Instead, it had two curtained windows with flowerboxes flanking a center door with an actual doorknob. It looked like a little cottage instead of a store. The sign above the door said *Perkins Apothecary*. Genevieve stopped in front.

"Do you want to get a soda?" she asked Lea.

Lea was parched. *All this walking, thinking, and talking really drain you.* She'd left her clothes and money at Genevieve's apartment, though—she couldn't buy a drink.

"Come on," Genevieve said, grabbing Lea by the elbow. "It'll be on the house."

"Okay, thanks," said Lea gratefully. "I'm really thirsty."

Lea expected that they would just grab bottles out of an ice chest, like at the general store, and drink them outside, but Genevieve walked to the back of the store and sat down on a stool at a counter. Lea followed and took the stool next to her. A boy of about sixteen was behind the counter. His face lit up when he saw Genevieve.

"Hi Genevieve," he said with a goofy smile. "I didn't know you were coming to the soda fountain today, but I'm sure glad you did."

"Hi Harold," answered Genevieve, looking just as silly.

They kept staring at each other and Lea wasn't sure if she should look away, clear her throat, or both. Finally, Genevieve remembered that Lea was there. "Harold, this is my new friend, Lea. Lea, this is Harold."

"Very pleased to meet you, Lea," Harold said politely.

"Hey," said Lea. "Same."

Genevieve and Harold both stared at Lea, confused. "Same as what?" asked Harold.

"Like, same here," said Lea, equally as confused. "As in…it's nice to meet you, too."

"Oh," said Harold. "Why didn't you say so?"

"I did," answered Lea.

Genevieve interrupted. "Harold, will you get us each a soda?" she asked, looking goofy again.

Harold hurriedly went to work, pouring Coke syrup and soda water from a fountain into two fancy glasses that looked to Lea like they should have ice cream sundaes in them instead of soda. He finished them off with glass straws that had small spoons on the end and placed them on napkins in front of the girls. The glass straws amazed Lea, but she didn't want to seem silly in front of Genevieve, so she decided not to make a big deal of them. Genevieve drank her soda, flirting with Harold the whole time.

"So, what do you think of my new dress?" Genevieve asked sweetly. Lea rolled her eyes and took another sip.

By the time Genevieve finished her drink, Lea was ready to throw up from the way she was batting her eyelashes. At last, Genevieve jumped off her stool.

"So, I'll pick you up at 7:30?" Harold asked.

"I'll be ready," Genevieve answered, cheesy smile still intact.

Genevieve and Lea left the apothecary and walked back toward the hardware store.

"I hope Harold will give me his ring tonight, so we can officially be a couple," said Genevieve wistfully.

"What do you mean by that? Do you want him to give you an engagement ring?" Lea asked, shocked.

Genevieve laughed. "No silly, his class ring. I can wear it as a necklace so everyone knows we're going steady."

This seemed strange to Lea. Some of her friends had older sisters with boyfriends, but no one wore anyone else's class ring as a necklace. She decided not to mention this to Genevieve. Instead, she changed the subject.

"I'm worried that we didn't pay for our Cokes," she said. "Is Harold going to pay for them?"

"Oh, it's Harold's family's apothecary," answered Genevieve. "I never have to pay."

The girls continued walking toward the hardware store. Lea's stomach started to growl. It must be getting close to dinner time. As the approached the hardware store, Genevieve said, "I have to go in for dinner now. Will you still be around tomorrow?"

"I don't know," answered Lea truthfully. "But I'll return your clothes now if you want."

"No, that's okay. Keep them. I have a feeling I'll be seeing you again."

Genevieve walked in the side door of the hardware store and Lea stood on the sidewalk, not sure of where to go. Main Street was quiet—most people had returned home for dinner. Lea had a lonely feeling that settled in the pit of her stomach, gnawing at her insides. She felt like crying, but held it in and swallowed around the dry lump in her throat. She remembered feeling like this once before when she was seven and she slept at Nicole's house for the first time. Lea had told Nicole's mom that she was sick, but Nicole's mom had assured Lea that she just missed home. The same thing was going on right now, she knew, but this time Lea didn't have anyone to help her through it. She had no idea if she would have any dinner, or where she would sleep. *Will I even get home—ever?*

The sick feeling in her stomach grew stronger. She decided to go to the park. At least she could sit there and not be obvious, and if she cried, no one would see.

As she walked to the back, Lea saw a swing set that she hadn't noticed before. She sat on a swing, going over her unbelievable day—and how she could find a way home.

The wind picked up, rustling her hair and blowing it into her eyes. She wiped the errant locks away. The swing started swaying back and forth, faster and faster—she grabbed hold of the swing—and higher and higher.

Lea gasped. It was happening again!

The wind pulled her in, flinging her violently through time and space. Lea shrieked in terror, but also in gratitude. She was going home!

The clouds gave way to sunshine and she found herself back on the farm, lying in the hammock.

"I'm home!" she gasped. "I'm safe!"

She looked toward the house. Dad stood at the grill and the rest of her family sat at the table on the deck, chatting while waiting for dinner. Lea jumped up from the hammock and stumbled as fast as she could across the back yard and onto the deck, excited to be back home. But as she sat in her chair at the table, everyone was staring at her.

"What are you wearing?" asked Sam. "You look like someone from *Grease*."

Lea looked down and was speechless. She was so excited to be back that she completely forgot about her clothes.

"Those are my clothes," Gramma said angrily. "You stole my clothes!"

Tears started to roll down Gramma's cheeks, and all attention turned her way. Lea used this diversion to run upstairs to change and come up with an excuse for her outfit. Could she tell her family that she had traveled back in time to 1953? There was no way anyone would believe her. By the time she returned to the deck, Gramma had calmed down and dinner was on the table.

Crisis averted.

It wasn't until after Gramma went back to bed that Lea's outfit was brought up again. This time it was Mom. "So what was with your outfit today?"

"I was at Nicole's and we got into an old box in the attic," Lea said, using the story she invented. "We were just messing around. I knew I was running late, so I just wore it home."

Lea's mom looked skeptical, but let it go.

Later, alone in her room, Lea tried to understand her very unusual day. If she hadn't arrived back in present time dressed in clothes from 1953, even she wouldn't believe that any of it had actually happened.

Why was I transported back in time? She didn't think that it was just a random trip. There had to be a reason. There was something there that she needed to see or know about—she just knew it.

Her mind was settled. She would go back to the hammock tomorrow and see if it would once again transport her to 1953.

CHAPTER FOUR

Tuesday morning Lea was up and dressed early, her backpack filled with Genevieve's clothes and some cash. She was in the kitchen toasting a waffle when her mom walked in.

"Good morning, honey," Mom said, greeting Lea with a kiss on her forehead. "I forgot to tell you yesterday, but I have an appointment at 10:00 and Sam has a football clinic. I need you to watch Gramma and the twins until I get home. I hope to be back by 12:00 or 1:00."

Lea stomped her foot. "*Mom!* I have stuff I want to do today! Why do I always have to watch Gramma? She doesn't even like me." She hated the sound of her whining voice, but she couldn't help it—when it came to watching Gramma, it just happened.

"I'm sorry I didn't give you any notice, but I need your help. I understand that having Gramma here is difficult, but she needs us. And Gramma loves you. She's just confused and scared so she takes it out on us. Besides, even if Gramma didn't live here, you would still have to watch Michael and Emily. You can have the afternoon to yourself."

"Fine," Lea muttered, as if she had a choice. She ate her waffle and hurried off to take care of the horses before Mom left. As she brushed Starburst, she thought more about Gramma accusing Lea of stealing her clothes. No matter what she did, she always managed to upset Gramma. Lea sighed, frustrated with her disappointments.

Lea was back at the house at 9:30, giving her mom and Sam just enough time to get out of the house on time. The twins were in the family room watching TV and Gramma was in the den. After checking to make sure the door to the sun porch was locked—she wasn't going to make that mistake again—Lea went to the kitchen to get some water. She could hear Gramma talking to her from the den.

"You have some nerve stealing my clothes, young lady."

Gramma remembered what happened last night? Lea was surprised. Gramma never remembered anything that happened that recently. She walked into the den, hopeful that maybe Gramma would remember more, but she was back to staring out the window, reciting lines.

Mom returned home at 1:00, just as Gramma, the twins, and Lea were finishing peanut butter and jelly sandwiches. Lea perked up when she heard the truck coming up the driveway. She quickly grabbed her backpack and threw it out on the deck. As soon as Mom walked through the kitchen door, Lea got up to leave out the back.

"Going for a hike and probably to the creek," she said, being as vague as possible in case Nicole or another friend happened to stop by. If Nicole wanted to get in touch with Lea badly enough and Lea wasn't answering her text messages, Nicole might get on her bike and ride over. The little white lie about going to the creek should avoid any snafus. Time travel wasn't easily explained to friends or parents. "I'll be home for dinner," she said, then added to herself, *At least, I hope I'll be home by then.* Lea rushed out the door before Mom could ask any questions, grabbing her backpack off the deck.

Lea ran to the hammock. Taking a quick glance to make sure no one was around, she ducked into the woods behind some brush and changed into Genevieve's clothes. She had no idea if the hammock would again transport her back in time or not, but she had to try.

She put her money in the pocket of the skirt, hid her backpack behind a tree, and lay down on the hammock. At first nothing happened.

Oh no! Lea thought. *What if I can't get back?*

She had panicked too early. The wind began to pick up and the hammock began to sway. Soon, Lea was back in the cloud twisting and turning through time. She squeezed her eyes shut and waited. In moments she was back on Main Street in 1953.

She grinned, giddy with her new secret. Now, she knew, she could easily move back and forth in time.

Lea wasn't sure where to go first. She wanted to find out why she was time traveling, but didn't have any leads. She started walking toward the park, hoping that she would find a clue.

The park was much busier today, filled with moms and young kids sitting on blankets in front of a small platform. Were they waiting for a show to start? Lea walked a little farther back so she was behind the platform. The actors were there, making last-minute adjustments to their costumes. As Lea got closer she recognized a face. *Genevieve!*

Genevieve waved to Lea. "I knew you'd be back! Come here, I want you to meet my friends." Genevieve gathered her friends and said, "Everyone, this is Lea."

"Hi, hello," they said in unison. Genevieve introduced Lea to a tall girl named Patty and a very pretty girl named Mary Jean. Mary Jean had brown eyes, but they were a different color brown than Lea had ever seen before—the color of caramel candy.

The boy who had helped Lea in front of Donnelly Park came walking up.

"Oh, and this is my brother," Genevieve added, pointing to him. Lea gave a wave, surprised that they were related.

"Are you staying for the show?" Genevieve asked. "You can come for sodas with us afterward."

"Sure," answered Lea.

Lea went out front and found a spot on the grass. Genevieve walked onto the platform and the crowd got quiet. Once she was sure she had everyone's attention. Genevieve began to speak.

"Good afternoon and welcome to Plays in the Park by the Cabot Corner Players. Today we are pleased to present *High School Troubles*, written by yours truly, Genevieve Clark. Please relax and enjoy the show."

The story line was about two high school friends who liked the same boy, who was played by Genevieve's brother. It poked fun at the girls for letting a boy come between them. In the last scene, the girls saw the boy buying a box of chocolates, and each assumed that it was for them, which led to an argument over which of them would receive it. The friends exchanged silly insults back and forth, only to find out that the boy bought the candy as a gift for his mother. In the end, the girls decided that their friendship was more important than the boy. As the curtain closed and the actors took a bow, Lea applauded, finding the play funny and very entertaining. Lea was impressed that Genevieve had written it, and also had to admit that she was a good actress.

Once the play was over, the park cleared out quickly. Lea stayed in the cool grass waiting for Genevieve and her friends to gather their props.

"Come on Lea," Genevieve said. "We're going to the apothecary."

On their walk, Genevieve pulled something out of her pocket. "Guess what I have in my hand?" she asked excitedly. Patti and Mary Jean both gasped and clapped, but Lea was confused.

"Did Harold ask you to go steady?" asked Patty.

"Did he give you his ring?" Mary Jean added.

Genevieve opened her hand and proudly showed them Harold's class ring on a chain. She put the necklace on and let the girls admire it.

"Well it's about time!" said Patty. "You two have been an unofficial couple *only* since second grade!"

Genevieve laughed and nudged Mary Jean. "Well, I guess, except for that time when Mary Jean tried to take him away from me. I think Harold had a crush on you back then. Not only were you the pretty new girl, you liked to climb trees and ride horses."

Mary Jean turned bright red. "I did *not* try to take him away from you! I had just moved here and I didn't know anyone. Harold was the first person I met, so I went over his house all the time. We were just friends. Besides, I was a tomboy back then. It was more fun to play in the fields with Harold and his friends than to play paper dolls with all of you."

They stopped outside the apothecary. Genevieve led the way to the back of the store and all the girls took a stool. Harold dutifully got each of them a soda, but it was clear that all he really wanted to do was talk to Genevieve. Even though Mary Jean was so pretty, Lea doubted that Harold had ever liked her as anything other than a friend—but if he had, it didn't matter. He clearly only had eyes for Genevieve.

The girls drank their sodas and said goodbye to Harold. Outside of the apothecary, Patty and Mary Jean left for home, leaving Genevieve and Lea alone.

"I really liked the play," Lea said as they started their walk toward the center of town.

"Thanks," answered Genevieve. "We started our theater group last summer. We take turns writing the scripts and we put on a play every week in the summer. They're a big hit, and we all have fun."

The girls were back at the hardware store, and it was time for Genevieve to go inside for dinner.

"What are you doing tomorrow?" Genevieve asked. "It's supposed to be hot. I can take you to the creek where we swim. I have an extra bathing suit you can wear."

Lea wasn't sure how to answer. What was her purpose for being here, in 1953? Was she meant to spend time with Genevieve? She liked Genevieve and wanted to get to know her better. "I think I can do that," she answered. It was fun having a friend in a different time.

"Meet me outside the hardware store at 1:00," Genevieve instructed before she went inside.

Lea made her way to the swing set in the park, feeling confident that it would bring her back home. Just as it was last evening, the park was again empty now. She sat on a swing and waited. Slowly and then more quickly, the wind came, snatching Lea into the cloud of time that had become her own personal transport service.

She was back in the hammock.

She ducked behind a tree and changed into her own clothes, smiling at her own little time travel secret. She threw her backpack over her shoulder and started toward the house, amazed with the time travel magic that had so suddenly come into her life.

Lea expected that her parents would be making dinner, but only Sam and Gramma were home.

"Where is everybody?" she asked Sam as she walked into Gramma's room.

"The twins have a baseball game tonight. There's pizza, though. And Nicole stopped by a little while ago. She tried to text you all afternoon, but you didn't respond. She's going to the lake with her family until Sunday. She just wanted you to know."

Lea nodded and grabbed a slice of pizza to bring upstairs. It was lucky that Nicole was going to the lake. It would have been tough to dodge her again tomorrow. Sometimes things just worked out, but Lea doubted this was just a coincidence. The time travel magic was hard at work for some reason. Lea just hoped that it would stick and that her mom wouldn't need help with Gramma or the twins tomorrow. She was looking forward to spending the afternoon with Genevieve.

Wednesday morning was cloudy with rain showers, which worried Lea. It was easy to be gone all afternoon on a sunny day without Mom thinking it was strange, but that wasn't so in the rain. But once she got downstairs Lea realized the weather wouldn't be a problem. Mom was getting Gramma ready to go out, and it looked like the twins were going too.

"Where are you all going?" Lea asked.

"Gramma has an appointment in the city and we're going to play with Auntie Michelle," Emily said with excitement.

Every few months Gramma went to see an Alzheimer's specialist in the city. Mom's sister also lived there. She would watch the twins while Mom took Gramma to the doctor, and after that they would have lunch. It was an all-day event, which meant that Lea's trip to the creek with Genevieve in 1953 wasn't in jeopardy because of the current weather.

"Where's Sam?" Lea asked.

"He's over at Jeremy's," Mom answered. "They're going to the indoor go-carts and the arcade today. I don't think he'll be home until dinner."

Lea couldn't believe her good fortune. *This time travel magic has to be real.*

In the barn, Lea mucked the stalls quickly and brushed the horses just enough to say that she did it. She felt a little guilty not taking Starburst for a ride; she hadn't spent any time with her this week. But right now Lea was more focused on 1953 than the present. She wasn't meeting Genevieve until 1:00, but since she had all day to herself, she decided to go back to 1953 early. She didn't want to waste a minute of the adventure.

Lea ran back to the house, packed her backpack, and grabbed a granola bar on her way out the door, eating it on the way to the hammock. She changed into Genevieve's clothes, hid her backpack, and lay down in the hammock. She waited for the wind.

Nothing. The air was still.

She closed her eyes and held on to the rope—but still, nothing happened. Lea sat up and changed her position so she was lying in the opposite direction, but the wind refused to cooperate. Lea swung the hammock, building up momentum back and forth, hoping it would trigger whatever force activated the time travel.

Still nothing. The air was completely still, but the rain was picking up. It began to pour. Lea grabbed her backpack and ran to the house, soaking wet.

Dad and the farm hands were talking and laughing in the kitchen. Normally she wouldn't have thought anything about this because Dad and his crew often had coffee in the kitchen during rainstorms, but she was wearing Genevieve's clothes. She could change in the yard, but there wasn't anywhere hidden enough. She tried to sneak in the front door, but realized that there was no way someone wouldn't see her before she got upstairs. Her best option was to run back by the hammock and change in the woods.

She peeled off Genevieve's clothes, trading them in for her own that were only damp, thanks to the protection of her backpack. She threw the drenched blob of Genevieve's clothes into her pack and turned, heading toward the house as the wind picked up, knocking Lea off balance. She stumbled over a rock and lost her footing, falling stomach first across the width of the hammock, her arms and legs dangling, her backpack falling to the ground.

As soon as her weight hit the hammock it began to swing higher and higher. *It's happening!* Lea thought, half exhilarated, half panicked.

Seconds later, Lea was flying through the air and through time, eventually landing on Main Street, Cabot Corner, 1953. Her modern clothes were damp and wrinkled, her hair was sopping wet, and she was barefoot, having lost her flip-flops mid-flight. Whatever magical force had overtaken her life must either be very mean or very funny, or maybe both.

Getting off Main Street was the best thing to do given her appearance. She ran down the alley by the hardware store to the fountain and literally bumped into Mary Jean.

Mary Jean blinked, stunned. Then she recognized Lea, and a look of confusion washed over her face. "Hi Lea, what on earth are you wearing? Where are your shoes, and why is your hair so wet?"

Lea plunked down on the bench, not knowing if she should laugh or cry. At the same time, Genevieve came down the alley. "You have *more* clothes like that?" Genevieve asked Lea.

"Actually, most of my clothes are like this. Sorry, I don't have your clothes today. It's kind of a long story."

"It's okay," Genevieve said slowly. "I have more you can borrow. But it's too early to go to the creek. Mary Jean and I were just going to figure out what to do with these things. Maybe you can help us." Genevieve held up two large wooden circles that reminded Lea of hula hoops. "My dad got some bins for the store and these were on top of them. He doesn't need them so I took them. I think we can use them in one of our plays. I just don't know how."

Genevieve started using one of them like a jump rope and Mary Jean was trying to twirl the other around her arm; neither was having much luck.

"Can I use one?" asked Lea. Mary Jean handed hers to Lea. She put it around her waist and started hula hooping. Genevieve's eyes lit up, and Mary Jean gasped.

"Let me try that!"

They both tried to imitate Lea with the other hoop, and at first weren't very successful. But after watching Lea and practicing a bit, they got the hang of it. The three spent the morning playing with the hoops and trying to come up with a script that would incorporate their new pastime.

At noon, Mary Jean went home for lunch, promising to meet Genevieve and Lea at the creek afterward. Genevieve and Lea walked upstairs to the apartment, where Genevieve made them a sandwich. Bologna on white bread wasn't what Lea usually ate, but she had to admit that it tasted pretty good. Gramma liked bologna sandwiches and white bread, she remembered suddenly, but Mom thought it was unhealthy, so she rarely bought it. Lea stopped mid-chew. For the first time, Lea thought about it from Gramma's point of view. *It must be hard to be an adult and still have someone else always decide what you're going to eat.*

"We should probably get changed and head to the

creek," Genevieve said. Lea nodded and brought her plate over to the sink, looking for a dishwasher.

"What are you looking for?" Genevieve asked.

"Where's your dishwasher?"

"I'm the dishwasher," Genevieve said, laughing. "But I'll just do them tonight with the dinner dishes. C'mon, let's get changed."

They walked into Genevieve's bedroom and Genevieve pulled two bathing suits out of a drawer. Lea's was pink with white flowers, and it looked more like a romper than a bathing suit. Once Lea was changed, Genevieve handed her something that looked like a bathrobe. "What's this?" Lea asked.

"It's a cover-up. We can't walk to the creek in just bathing suits," Genevieve answered as if it was silly for Lea to consider anything otherwise. *What would Genevieve think about the bikinis that my friends and I wear?* She smiled to herself. Genevieve would not approve. They grabbed two towels from a hallway closet and the girls headed out the door.

Mary Jean, Patty, and a few other teenagers were at the creek when Genevieve and Lea arrived. A couple of the boys were in the water, but the girls were sitting on the grass. Lea sat down next to Mary Jean, but Genevieve didn't. She took off her cover-up, threw it on the ground, and ran to a rope swing hanging from a tree. The next thing Lea knew, Genevieve was swinging over the water and letting go. She landed with a splash, spraying the boys with water. Genevieve and the rest of the girls were laughing, but Lea was too surprised to join in. Genevieve seemed so proper and lady-like; she never expected her to fly into the water from a swing.

"C'mon Lea," Genevieve called. "Try the rope swing."

Lea didn't have to be asked twice. She and her present-day friends also loved using the rope swing. She pulled off her cover-up and ran to the swing, and in seconds she can-nonballed next to Genevieve in the water. The other girls waded in. It wasn't long before everyone was in the water, splashing, swimming, and laughing.

"Lea, I bet I can swing farther into the creek than you can," Genevieve challenged as she climbed out of the water and ran to the swing. Before Lea could answer, Genevieve was high on the rope, swinging out so far that Lea thought she was going to land on the other side of the creek. But just in time, the swing came back enough and Genevieve land-ed in the water. Everyone laughed and declared Genevieve Queen of the Rope. The rest of the afternoon was filled with games of Marco Polo, contests to see who could hold their breath the longest underwater, and laughing.

It was around 3:30 when a few clouds began to roll in. The boys were the first to leave and then Genevieve, Mary Jean, Patty, and Lea began putting on their cover-ups.

"Do you want to stop by my house to meet Star?" Mary Jean asked Lea.

"Who's Star?" Lea asked.

"The best horse in the world," answered Genevieve.

Lea gasped. "Yes!" she said excitedly. "I love horses. Mine is named Starburst."

The girls all looked at Lea skeptically. "Oh, I mean, in the future if I have a horse, I want to name it Starburst," she said, remembering they all thought she was poor.

Mary Jean said, "Well let's go then!"

The girls walked down a country road that Lea knew well, and stopped in Mary Jean's driveway—*Lea's* driveway. The sign in front stated *Landry Farm*. That might have been true in 1953, but in present this was the Grant Farm, her family's farm.

Lea was amazed to see the 1953 version of her house. Even from the outside it was clear the farmhouse would be renovated and rooms would be added in the years between Mary Jean's family occupied the house and it would be the Grants' house, but still, standing in her future driveway, staring at the house that her family would own decades later, Lea felt deeply connected to Mary Jean. She looked at the girl with caramel eyes, wanting to tell her that this was her future home, and ask to go inside and look around. Lea stayed quiet, knowing that neither Mary Jean nor Genevieve and Patty would understand.

Lea followed the other girls as they walked out back toward the barn, although she could have found it by herself with her eyes closed. She smiled to herself when she noticed a hammock hanging in the backyard near where Lea's family had their hammock. The Grants' barn was much bigger than the one belonging to Mary Jean's family, but it was set up the same way. A basket of carrots and apples hung just inside the barn door, just like in the present. The girls grabbed some carrots took turns feeding Star.

"Maybe another day we can ride," Genevieve suggested.

"You ride?" Lea asked Genevieve.

"Mary Jean taught me," she answered. "I love it."

As much as Lea was enjoying her time with the girls and Star, she could see the clouds thickening. It was bound to rain soon. Genevieve noticed too.

"We should head back to town," she said. When the girls said goodbye, Patty continued down the country road to her house while Genevieve and Lea walked in the opposite direction to the hardware store. It was strange for Lea to walk away from the farm, knowing she was doing so to get back home. She glanced back as she and Genevieve walked down the road.

"I think I'd like living on a farm," Genevieve said when she noticed Lea looking back.

Lea just smiled at Genevieve and answered, "Yes."

The clouds were dark and thick by the time Lea and Genevieve got back to Main Street. They hurried to the apartment to change. Genevieve's parents were still working in the hardware store, but her brother was home, reading a comic book in the living room.

Lea changed back into her clothes that she had left at Genevieve's the first time she visited 1953 and put her wrinkled clothes from earlier in a bag.

"I don't want your brother to see me in these clothes," she said to Genevieve.

"Just wear my cover-up," Genevieve suggested.

Lea had already put the one she had worn in a laundry basket that was next to Genevieve's bed, so she grabbed the cover-up that Genevieve wore and put it on.

"Well, I guess I should head out. Thanks for a fun day. Maybe we can ride Star sometime soon."

"Yes," answered Genevieve. "Let's do that next week. I have plans for the next few days."

"With Harold?" Lea teased.

"Yes," answered Genevieve, unable to conceal a large smile. "He doesn't have to work on Thursday or Friday, and then it's the weekend."

Lea left Genevieve and hurried to the park. The wind was picking up and it was starting to rain. She got to the park just as a bolt of lightning cracked overhead. Lea ran to the swings and sat down.

She had barely sat when she was lifted into a cloud. The twisting and turning seemed faster than normal and she found herself suddenly back in the hammock. The backpack she had dropped earlier was still on the ground. It was starting to rain lightly in the present too, and the sky was a greenish gray that meant a thunderstorm was imminent. She opened her backpack and threw her bag of wet clothes into it, then she took off Genevieve's cover-up and was about to put that in the pack when something hit her foot.

She looked down. *Harold's class ring!* Genevieve had put it in the pocket of her cover-up when they were swimming. Lea had to get the ring back!

Lea lay down on the hammock, hoping the wind would carry her back to 1953. The wind was blowing hard, but it wasn't time travel wind—it was storm wind, and it was blowing branches off trees. A large branch from the old maple that supported one end of the hammock came crashing down, barely missing Lea. She gasped and jumped up, knowing she had to get inside. Clutching the ring in one hand and her backpack in the other, she ran to the house.

Dad was in the kitchen making dinner when Lea came running in, but no one else was home yet.

"Where have you been, Lea?" he asked. "I was starting to get worried. This storm has been brewing all day."

"Sorry, Dad. I was just out exploring. I went to the creek, and then I visited the horses." This satisfied her dad, and Lea felt justified that she hadn't technically lied. She was just grateful that her mom wasn't home.

Lea went upstairs and put Harold's ring in the top drawer of her dresser. She would return it to Genevieve first thing in the morning. Lea knew she would be missing it.

As Lea returned to the kitchen, Mom, Gramma, and the twins were arriving home from the city. The calm of the day quickly turned to chaos as the twins entered the house. They were excited, each talking over the other as they told Dad and Lea about their adventures in the park with Aunt Michelle. They dumped a bag of rocks they had collected all over the kitchen table, and said they had enjoyed ice cream, more of which appeared to be on Emily's shirt than in her stomach. Aunt Michelle had gotten each of them "invisible dogs" that were "attached" to plastic collars held by wire leashes. Michael was now using his to bop Emily on the head as she ran around the table to get away from him. Mom was trying to get Gramma to sit down at the table without falling over the twins, and Dad and Lea were dodging all of them in an attempt to stay out of the way.

A loud crack of thunder sounded, and the zigzag of lightning lit up the dark gray sky. An instant later they heard a loud bang, and the eerie quiet of a sudden power outage overtook the kitchen. For a moment, no one moved or said a word, and then a second chaos erupted. The twins started whining that they wouldn't be able to watch TV or play video games, Mom and Dad were opening and closing drawers and closets looking for candles and flashlights, and Gramma began to cry. Lea went to Gramma's side and helped her out of the kitchen chair.

"C'mon Gramma, let's go into your room."

Gramma went with Lea, quietly crying the whole time. "This is just terrible," she said to Lea through her tears. "The damage to the store was awful. The damage everywhere was so bad. And then I couldn't find it in the darkness."

Lea wasn't sure what Gramma was talking about, but she patted her hand to try to calm her down. "Don't worry, Gramma. The lights will come back on soon."

It took a few minutes, but Mom and Dad lit candles and distributed flashlights, and the twins cleared the kitchen table of their rock collection. Gramma and Lea rejoined the family in the kitchen. Dad had finished cooking dinner before the power went out, and everyone sat down to enjoy the meal. The storm passed and the early evening summer sun popped out from behind a cloud. Before dinner was over, the power was back on.

Sam came bounding into the kitchen, breathless. "The big maple by the pasture got hit by lightning! It cracked right in half. The hammock is ripped and there are branches everywhere."

What? Lea's heart seized. If the hammock was ripped, how was she going to get Harold's ring back to Genevieve?

Lea ran out the door and into the backyard. Sam was right: The old maple had been mangled by the storm and the hammock had been ripped in half, each side still attached to the tree on either side. How was she going to get back to 1953?

The morning after a big storm was always beautiful in Cabot Corner, and Thursday was no exception. Wednesday's thick humidity had given way to bright sunshine and a crisp blue sky. Lea did her chores early and made her way to the remains of the hammock before any of the farmhands had a chance to throw it away and cut down the old maple. She carried the ring in the pocket of her shorts just in case she could get back to Genevieve.

Lea sat down on the half of the hammock that was attached to the destroyed maple. Even though the hammock was on the ground, she hoped that something might happen. It didn't. Then she tried the other half of the hammock that was tied to a living tree. Still nothing. Lea tied the hammock back together, but her knots weren't tight enough to support her weight. When she sat on the semi-repaired hammock, she fell right through to the ground, the hammock again in two pieces.

The twins' swing set—maybe the swing set will work.

She walked to the backyard and sat on a swing. That didn't work, so she tried the one next to it, and even tried pumping it a little to get things going. Nothing.

It seemed like the time travel magic had been washed away in last night's storm.

Dejected, Lea walked back to the house. Inside, Gramma was sitting in her chair with an old photo album opened in her lap. Mom was kneeling next to her, talking to Gramma about the pictures.

"What are you guys doing?" Lea asked.

Mom looked up. "Yesterday the doctor suggested that it might help Gramma to look at old photo albums, so I pulled these out. Maybe later you can look at some with her."

Lea nodded and went to her room. Right now she was only concerned about getting Harold's ring back to Genevieve. Sitting on her bed, she thought about other ways she might get back to 1953. Donnelly Park in 2019 didn't have a swing set, but there was a new playground a little farther up Main Street. Maybe the swings there would take her back to Genevieve? The playground on a beautiful summer day would be packed, though, and time travel seemed to require both solitude and secrecy. Lea finally decided that she would just ask her parents to get another hammock.

Lea went back downstairs and found Mom in the kitchen. "Do you think we could go get another hammock today?" she asked her mom.

"Sure. I have to go to Walmart in a little while. We can look there."

⁓

An hour later, Lea, Mom, and Gramma were in the Suburban heading to Walmart. "I think we need to take Gramma out more," Mom told Lea during the ride. "She never sees anyone except us. She probably gets bored."

This worried Lea. Bringing Gramma out was a lot of work, and it never went well. She tended to insult people, especially anyone she thought didn't look "appropriate." But Lea also had to laugh a little at this. Gramma lived mostly in the past, and after traveling back in time, Lea was more sympathetic about not understanding what was acceptable or unacceptable depending on the decade. *It must be strange for Gramma to see the world now when she thinks it's still 1953.*

Mom went to the pharmacy to pick up a prescription for Gramma, so Lea was in charge of making sure that Gramma was safe. Lea tried to bring her to the outdoor supply section to find the hammocks, but on the way, they passed the toy section. A hula hoop display at the end of an aisle caught Gramma's eye. She picked one up, and in no time she was swinging it around her waist like she was a hula hoop champion. Lea laughed at the sight of an old woman swinging her hips to keep the hoop moving, and had to admit it was impressive to watch—but she was also a little embarrassed. It wasn't long before a few people started watching and then a crowd began to form. Gramma was a hit!

As the small crowd applauded and cheered, Gramma took a bow and smiled at Lea. Lea's heart warmed—it was the first time she could remember Gramma smiling at her. When Gramma put the hula hoop back, they continued toward the outdoor supply section.

Lea couldn't find a hammock anywhere. The department clerk explained that they were sold out until next year, dashing Lea's hopes of getting back to 1953 that afternoon.

"I'll order one online," Mom offered when she caught up to them. "It will here by the end of the week."

Lea nodded and they started back toward the checkout. As they passed the toy section, Lea asked, "Can we get a hula hoop?"

Mom looked at Lea like she had sprouted another head.

"I just thought it might be fun," Lea reasoned.

"Sure," Mom answered. "Why not?"

Gramma smiled at Lea again.

They walked to the car. Not only did Gramma's visit to Walmart go okay, but it was actually fun. Lea smiled, surprised and grateful.

It was noon when they got back home. Mom made lunch for Lea, Sam, the twins, and Gramma. Gramma wanted bologna, but turkey was the only deli meat that Mom ever bought.

"Mom, will you buy some bologna next week?" Lea asked.

"Do you like bologna?" Mom asked back. "When have you ever had it?"

Lea stumbled with her answer. "Um, Nicole's mom sometimes buys it," she lied. "It isn't bad, and Gramma is always asking for it."

"Well, Gramma isn't supposed to have it, but I guess once in a while it would be okay. If I buy it though, you better eat it."

And Gramma smiled at Lea again.

After lunch, Sam left to go to the fishing hole with Jeremy, and the twins started asking about going to the town beach. Lea escaped to the backyard where she could be alone and try to figure out how to get back to 1953. There was no way to get the ring back to Genevieve unless the time travel magic returned, and Lea had no control over that.

She could hear Emily and Michael laughing as she walked back to the house, and she followed the sound to the back deck where Gramma was putting on a show with the hula hoop. Lea smiled when she saw that Gramma was still enjoying their new purchase. Gramma was able to keep the hula hoop going for quite a while, and she clapped in delight at her accomplishment. When the hula hoop finally dropped to the ground, Mom called them all inside.

"Lea, I know this is short notice, but will you watch Gramma for a few hours? The twins want to go to the town beach. It's such a nice day, I don't want to tell them no."

"It's okay. My plans for the afternoon didn't work out anyway."

Mom and the twins left for their outing and Gramma made her way to her chair and sat down. She fell asleep in a few minutes, most likely tired from the trip to Walmart and all the hula hooping. Lea wasn't sure what to do. She didn't want to turn on the TV and risk waking Gramma, and she certainly wasn't leaving her alone after what happened the last time.

Lea sat in the chair next to Gramma and started flipping through the photo albums that Mom had pulled out. There were photos of Mom and Aunt Michelle as teenagers and little girls, and a bunch of pictures of people that Lea didn't recognize. Lea hoped to see some pictures of Gramma, but there weren't any in this album. She closed the album and found another one in the pile with *High School* written in marker on the front. She picked it up and tried to open it, but the cover wouldn't budge. It seemed to be glued shut.

As Lea tried to pry to cover away from the first page, the album began glowing with a golden hue. Stunned by the sudden glow, Lea recoiled, dropping it on the floor. She stared in awe as the light grew brighter and the cover let loose, popping open by itself on the floor. Lea's curiosity overtook her shock. As she bent over to get a closer look at the still-glowing book, Lea was sucked headfirst into the album. It opened into a tunnel.

She screamed, diving deeper and deeper into nothingness—helpless. She was twisting and swirling through the dark and narrow passage, led by the golden light. Finally, the tunnel widened and the darkness gave way to the light.

Lea was suddenly upright, standing on Main Street, Cabot Corner, 1953, next to the same bench where she always arrived.

Lea had been trying all morning to get back to 1953, but now that she was there, all she wanted was to get back to the present. She was supposed to be watching Gramma! Mom and the twins were at the town beach and Sam was fishing with Jeremy. Dad was working on the farm, but he wouldn't be inside for hours. There was no telling how long Gramma would sleep or what she would do if she woke up.

She bolted toward Donnelly Park. She had to get to the swing set.

Something didn't seem right. It was a beautiful day, but there was no one around at the park. Trees everywhere were toppled over. The rainstorm that was starting when she left 1953 yesterday must have turned into a storm, like the one they had last night in the present.

Her heart sank when she reached the swing set. A huge tree had fallen right across it. The cross bar was broken in the middle and the swings lay helplessly on the ground. Lea stared in despair. How would she get back? And more importantly, was Gramma okay? She felt a pang in her stomach wondering if Gramma was still sleeping or if she had wandered off somewhere.

Lea sank to her knees, unsure of what to do next. As she sat, the felt Harold's ring press into her leg. *Maybe the best thing to do is to find Genevieve and return the ring.* Perhaps if she returned the ring, a way back would appear. After all, the photo album had sucked her in to get her back to 1953 rather suddenly. There must be a reason. Maybe if she figured that reason out, she would be transported back to take care of Gramma.

Lea jumped up and started for the hardware store. There weren't many people out today, so she felt less self-conscious about her clothes and about running through town. As she continued up Main Street though, she realized why people weren't in the stores and restaurants. The swing set wasn't the only thing that had been damaged. Lea had been in such a hurry to get to the park that she hadn't noticed the damage to Main Street. Benches were knocked over. Trees rested on top of buildings. The stores that hadn't been damaged were open, but they didn't appear to have electricity. A steady stream of customers walked in and out of the hardware store—most were buying what appeared to be building supplies, most likely to make repairs. Genevieve wasn't in the store, but Lea saw her brother was helping out. Lea didn't want to be noticed. She had never met Genevieve's parents, and although she knew Genevieve's brother, she wasn't dressed appropriately to say hello.

Lea walked to the courtyard in back of the store hoping that Genevieve might be there. She wasn't. *What to do next?* Lea sat on the bench to think. Genevieve had told her that Harold wasn't working today and that they had plans, but she never mentioned what those plans were. They couldn't be at the movies because there was no electricity, but maybe they went to the creek.

Lea started along the quiet country road that led there, noticing how different Cabot Corner was in 1953. Trees and meadows occupied the land now taken up by restaurants, grocery stores, gas stations, and mini-mall plazas. Few cars passed during her walk. In the present this was one of the busiest roads in Cabot Corner. It was the place where everyone went to shop and eat. But now, it was peaceful.

As she turned off the country road onto the dirt road leading to the creek, she could hear the water. Instead of the usual quiet bubbling, there was a rushing sound. Lea was surprised to see the creek overflowing its banks, flooding some of the land around it. There were trees down everywhere.

It seemed strange to Lea that there were such big storms

on the same night in both 1953 and in present time. Lea looked around a little, but quickly realized that there was no one swimming today. The water flow was too strong, and the flooding and downed trees left nowhere to sit.

Her thoughts returned to Gramma as Lea began the trek back to Main Street. Lea hoped she was okay. And for the first time since she was back in 1953, Lea worried about what Mom was going to think if she and the twins got home before Lea got back. Her mother would never believe that she had been sucked into the photo album and brought back to 1953, and Lea really couldn't blame her. Lea just hoped that she would return first. That was the only option. But since she couldn't find Genevieve, how was she to get back home?

Back on Main Street, Lea stopped by the apothecary—perhaps Genevieve and Harold were having a soda. But as she got closer, she realized that the apothecary wasn't open. A tree rested across what was left of the roof, and the front door was lying on the sidewalk, blown off its hinges by storm wind the night before. Lea walked closer to see inside. The floor was flooded, but there were a couple of people bailing water out the side windows and a few others were collecting merchandise off shelves.

There they are!

It had taken Lea a moment to realize that Genevieve and Harold were the ones baling the water. Genevieve was wearing jeans, a T-shirt, and rubber fisherman boots. Her usually perfectly styled hair was pulled back in a thick headband. Lea wanted to call out to Genevieve, but she didn't want the other people in the apothecary to notice her. Lea had to get the ring to Genevieve, and then she had to get back to Gramma.

Lea picked her way to the side of the building. The trunk of the tree that had destroyed the apothecary roof was still standing, and a large lower branch was still intact. This branch nearly touched the apothecary window where Genevieve was tossing out water. Lea used a rock next to branch as a step stool, and pulled herself up onto the branch where she could try to get Genevieve's attention.

Just as she was about to call out, though, a gust of wind caused the branch to sway violently. It moved faster and faster until Lea was sure it would break from the tree. Lea lost her grip on the branch and began falling to the ground, but she never hit. Instead, the earth gave way to a dark tunnel and before Lea knew it, she was tumbling and twisting, back to the den where Gramma was still sound asleep in her chair.

Gramma was safe—Lea was relieved. But, she hadn't managed to give Genevieve the ring. It seemed that the time travel magic had a plan. She didn't know why she was transported back just to see the storm damage, but she doubted that the magic took her back so she could return Harold's ring. If that had been the reason, she would have had a chance to give it to Genevieve. She just hoped the chance would come.

CHAPTER
SEVEN

Lea was lost in thought about the storm in 1953 and she felt terrible about the damage to Harold's family business. The apothecary was a mess.

She also realized how much she didn't know about Genevieve. Before today, she had seen Genevieve mostly as prim and proper, and a little spoiled and vain. Other than the time they spent together at the creek, Genevieve dressed immaculately and everything else about her seemed perfect, too. But now, Lea kept seeing Genevieve in jeans and fishing boots, bailing water out of the apothecary window. It was a much different picture. There was much more to Genevieve than swinging on a rope swing and flirting with her boyfriend, Lea realized. She obviously cared about Harold and his family very much.

A cough from Gramma brought Lea back to the present. Startled, Lea looked up and saw that Gramma was smiling at her. And then Lea had an idea.

"Gramma, do you want to take a walk? It's a nice day."

Gramma's smile grew. "Yes."

Lea helped Gramma from her chair and they made their way to the back yard. Lea tried to lead Gramma in a circle around the perimeter of the yard, where the ground was more level, but Gramma wanted to walk into the pasture. They strolled along the path that led to the horse barn, Lea holding Gramma's hand on the uneven terrain.

"Where are the horses?" Gramma asked, obviously disappointed that they weren't outside.

"They're just in the barn," answered Lea. "They'll be out later."

"Well, I'd like to see them now," Gramma responded.

Gramma moved a little faster, heading toward the barn. Once inside, she went straight to Starburst's stall.

"Hello Star," she whispered to the horse.

Lea didn't remember talking to Gramma about Starburst, and she was surprised that she almost got her name right.

"Can I ride her?" Gramma asked.

Lea hesitated, not sure that Gramma on a horse was the best idea. Besides, what would Mom think? Gramma looked so happy, though, that Lea didn't want to disappoint her.

"How about if I lead you around the pasture?"

Gramma didn't answer, but her smile lit up the barn.

Lea had no idea how she would get Gramma onto Starburst, but she decided to try. She grabbed her saddle and secured it on Starburst, and then got a step stool to give Gramma a little more height. Gramma stepped up, put her left foot into the stirrup and swung her leg over Starburst's back like she did it every day. Before Lea could take the reins from Gramma, Gramma gently nudged Starburst and they started out of the barn at a light prance. Once they were out of the barn, Starburst picked up the pace to a trot. Lea knew she wouldn't be able to safely get the reins from Gramma, so she called to her, "You need to stay with me."

Gramma didn't stop Starburst, but they didn't go any faster, either. Lea watched, her stomach in knots, as Gramma and Starburst trotted in a circle around the barn. As she watched Gramma ride, her panic subsided and Lea realized that Gramma knew how to ride and that she was safe. Gramma finally stopped Starburst in front of Lea.

"Get a horse," Gramma said.

It took Lea a minute to process the words, but then they clicked. She ran into the barn and saddled Sam's horse, Patches. She rode out of the barn, and together Gramma and Starburst, and Lea and Patches began walking through the wooded trails that flanked the farm. Gramma led the way and seemed to be familiar with the path.

They made their way to the creek and rode along its bank, the waters still swollen from last night's storm. Branches were strewn about, but only one tree had fallen. Lea couldn't help but compare the creek as it looked right now to how it looked just a little while ago when she was in 1953. The water overflow and damage done by fallen trees today was nowhere near as bad.

They rode slowly, without any words exchanged, but as Lea watched Gramma on Starburst, she saw a side of her grandmother that she had never seen before. Instead of viewing Gramma as a sick old lady, she glimpsed her as someone who shared her love for horses. For the first time, Lea saw her as her grandmother—someone with whom she shared a connection and common interests.

Lea and Gramma returned to the house only a short time before Mom and the twins got back from the lake, but Gramma was already fast asleep in her chair.

"Did you and Gramma have a nice afternoon?" Mom asked.

Lea smiled. "Yes."

Now that Mom and the twins were back from the beach, Lea was no longer responsible for Gramma, which meant she could leave Gramma's side whenever she chose. Usually, Lea couldn't wait to get away, but today was different. She had enjoyed her recent interactions with Gramma, especially their horseback ride. She wanted to savor the bond that was growing between them because, to be honest, she wasn't sure it would last. With her Alzheimer's, Gramma was known for being unpredictable. And, of course, Lea was curious about the photo album that had acted as a portal back to 1953. Why had it been the link to the past—and would it work again? She had to at least try.

Lea waited until her mother was busy in another part of the house before she picked up the album. This time the cover easily opened and no golden hue illuminated the book. Instead, Lea was amazed by what she saw. There was a picture of Clark's Hardware Store and another of Perkins' Apothecary! On another page was a picture of a party being held in Donnelly Park.

Look at all these familiar places, she thought. Then she realized, almost smacking her forehead, that Gramma had grown up in Cabot Corner. It made perfect sense. *Did Gramma know Genevieve or Mary Jean? Had they ever been friends?*

Emily interrupted Lea's thoughts, running breathlessly into the den.

"Will you come with me to Donnelly Park tonight to see the play on the grandstand? The middle school theater group is putting on *The Doll People*. Mom can drive us but she can't stay because she has to take Michael to football practice. Please, please, please? It's my favorite book."

Lea looked at her sister, but she was thinking of Genevieve and her theater group. Lea wondered if Gramma had ever seen any of their plays.

"Well?" asked Emily impatiently.

"Sure. But let's ask Mom if we can bring Gramma too. You know how she likes plays."

After a quick dinner, Mom, Gramma, Emily, Lea, and Michael and his football gear headed into town. Mom dropped Gramma and the girls off in front of the park.

"Lea, make sure you keep one eye on Emily and the other on Gramma," she said sternly. "I'll drop Michael off and be right back."

"Don't worry, Mom. We'll be fine."

Emily ran ahead toward the bandstand with a blanket and a bag of snacks while Lea, carrying two folding chairs, walked more slowly with Gramma. They sat down at the spot Emily chose, as close to the stage as they could get. Gramma seemed happy to be in the park, and sat patiently. Emily's friend Cassie had joined her on the blanket since her family had chosen to sit farther back. Lea relaxed a little now that they were situated and looked around the crowd to see if she recognized anyone in the audience. She spied her friend Trevor a few rows back, and started waving, trying to get his attention.

Lea was so focused on Trevor that she didn't notice that Gramma had left her chair, made her way up the grandstand stairs, and was now standing in the middle of the stage.

"Welcome to Plays in the Park…"

Whipping around, Lea was startled by Gramma's voice booming out across the crowd assembled in Donnelly Park. She jumped out of her seat and started toward the stage, but Mrs. Cooper, the middle school drama coach—whom Gramma had once accused of stealing from the church collection plate—got to Gramma first.

Mrs. Cooper didn't miss a beat. "And please welcome Mrs. Perkins, who is helping our theater group out tonight."

The audience applauded and Gramma bowed and beamed with joy.

Mrs. Cooper whispered something in Gramma's ear, and together, the women announced, "Enjoy our production of *The Doll People*!"

Gramma walked down the bandstand staircase with Mrs. Cooper and Lea met them at the bottom. "Thank you," said Lea, her cheeks flaming.

Mrs. Cooper smiled. "You and your grandmother are welcome to come out back with the cast. I think she might enjoy it. She was my drama coach when I was in high school. I learned so much from her. She was a wonderful actress, and she was a good playwright too!"

Emily was enjoying the show with Cassie, and Cassie's family was just a row or two behind them, so Lea agreed to stay backstage with Gramma. As Lea watched Gramma admire the props and try on some hats that were part of the costumes, she had a glimpse of what Gramma was like before Alzheimer's disease.

CHAPTER NINE

Friday morning brought the sun, but Gramma woke up grumpy. As happy as Gramma was the night before, her morning crankiness overshadowed it. There were no smiles for Lea when she checked in on Gramma after she did her chores, and even Sam was told to stay away from the chocolates.

"Gramma sure is in a bad mood today," Lea complained to Mom.

"She's been out a lot this week. She's tired. You've spent a lot of time with her the past few days. Why don't you take a break and go for a hike or something? I asked Sam to help out today, and I'll be home too."

Harold's ring, always in Lea's pocket, was digging into her leg. Maybe today she would be able to return it to Genevieve.

"Okay," said Lea. "I'm going for a hike in the woods."

She kissed her mom goodbye and headed out on what she hoped would be a productive adventure. Lea walked toward the creek, yearning that the time travel magic would find her and somehow whisk her back to 1953.

As she neared the rope swing, a gust of wind blew the rope high into the air and far out over the creek. The rope came back and flew out the same way again.

Is the magic calling to me? she wondered.

Lea grabbed the rope as it returned to the bank a third time. She wrapped her legs around it and sailed out over the water. This time, instead of returning to the bank, the rope began rotating like a tornado. Lea held on as long as she could, half fearful that this wasn't the time travel magic's doing, until the force of the motion caused her to lose her grip. Lea spun through the air—and landed next to the 1953 version of the creek.

Lea was surprised to land outside of town, but by now she knew that the magic always had a plan. Trees and stray branches still littered the landscape, but the creek water had receded to normal levels. Lea walked along the bank and then through the woods to the country road that would bring her into town. Her route brought her by the front of the Landry Farm, and curiosity overtook her. Lea's goal was to get Harold's ring back to Genevieve, but getting a better look at the farm as it was in 1953 wouldn't take very long.

Ducking behind the woods on the side lawn, Lea walked back toward the pasture where she could get a good look at the back of the house. The porch or deck hadn't been added on yet, so the house appeared to be much smaller. Her house in the present was white, but Mary Jean's family preferred red. The back yard was different too. The twins' swing set had replaced a vegetable garden, and there was a chicken coop next to that. Lea's family raised cattle and grew corn to sell, but they didn't keep chickens or grow their own vegetables. In 2019, farming for the Grants was business, but it looked like it was more of a way of life for Mary Jean's family.

Mary Jean came out the back door with a basket in her hand. She walked over to the garden and started picking vegetables. Lea had lived on a farm her entire life, but she had never picked a vegetable off a plant. Curiosity got the better of her once again.

"Mary Jean!" Lea yelled from the wooded area next to the back yard.

Mary Jean looked up, surprised. "Hi Lea. What are you doing over in the woods?"

"I was out for a walk. I went down near the swimming hole. I was curious to see how many trees were down."

"That was some storm, wasn't it? We were lucky not to have any damage on the farm. Harold's family is worried because there's so much damage to the apothecary. They won't be open for a while. Have you seen it?"

"I was on Main Street yesterday," Lea said. "It looked pretty bad."

"They have a lot of repairs to make before they can re-open. Genevieve's family is selling them supplies from the hardware store at cost, and members of the Elks Club are helping Mr. Perkins fix the roof. Genevieve has been there every day helping clean up the water damage."

Mary Jean started picking vegetables and putting them in the basket. Lea watched for a minute or two to see how it was done, and then she started to help.

"Do you think Genevieve is there today? I want to give her something."

Mary Jean shrugged. "I would imagine she is. I'm bringing the vegetables to town once I'm done picking. Do you want to walk with me?"

"Sure, but why are you bringing the vegetables to town?"

"The church is serving meals this week because so many people don't have electricity or have damage to their homes. My mom is helping with the cooking and we're donating the vegetables we grow for our family."

Working together, the girls filled Mary Jean's basket quickly and started walking toward town.

"Do you have a lot of chores on the farm?" Lea asked.

"I help take care of the horses, feed the chickens, and collect the eggs. I also have to do the dishes after dinner and help take care of my little sisters and brothers."

"Wow, that seems like a lot of work," Lea said.

"There's a lot of work to do on a farm," Mary Jean answered.

Lea nodded. Mary Jean had to do a lot more to help than she did.

"Do you have your own bedroom?"

"No, I share a room with my older sister, Joan, but we have the biggest room. It's in the back of the house, so it overlooks the pastures. I like to watch the cows and horses when they're outside."

Lea could tell from Mary Jean's description that she and Mary Jean had the same room.

Mary Jean continued, "The best thing about our room, though, is the little room in the back of the closet, under the eaves. Now that Joan is out of high school and working, she doesn't spend as much time there, but I still love it."

Lea smiled again, because she also loved that little room. Her extra-large beanbag chair and a small table took up most of the space, but she enjoyed sitting in there to listen to music or watch something on her laptop.

"On New Year's Eve three years ago, when it turned 1950, I made a time capsule. I put newspaper clippings and pictures of the farm, the town, and our family and friends in it, and I hid it in the wall. I cut out a piece of the plaster right underneath the window with one of Daddy's tools, and I stuck it behind a board. I put the plaster back almost perfectly, but if you look closely, you can see the cut marks. I hope that someday, someone will find it and know all about what life was like on the farm in 1950."

Lea was too stunned to say anything, but she didn't have time to anyway. The wind picked up. A dark cloud appeared and it surrounded Lea and Mary Jean. They could see each other—Mary Jean's eyes were wide with surprise and delight—but nothing around them. The cloud spun around them, taking both girls with it.

As Lea and Mary Jean tumbled through the air together, Lea understood what was happening, but she wasn't sure if Mary Jean did. Lea had come to view time travel as a solitary experience, so knowing that Mary Jean was spinning and flipping through time with her seemed strange. *What does Mary Jean think of all this? What might Mary Jean tell Genevieve?*

They landed on their feet, next to the creek at the swimming hole. Pouring rain and strong winds pulled Lea out of her thoughts. The first thing she noticed was how quickly the water was moving. The creek was swollen beyond its bank. Before either of them could mention time travel, or figure out to what year they had traveled, they heard a panicked voice struggling to be heard over the rushing water and heavy wind.

"Help! I'm stuck. Help me. Help me!"

The girls looked toward the creek and saw a boy of about seven or eight, his clothing soaked, standing on a large rock in the middle of the creek.

"I'm not a good swimmer and the water is deeper than usual," he cried. "The water keeps rising. Help me. I'm scared!"

Lea and Mary Jean looked at each other, not sure of what to do. The water was violent, and neither was sure how deep it was. Lea noticed that the rope swing hung in its usual place.

"We can use the rope swing," Lea said. "If we tie it around a thick downed branch, I can put it underneath me, like a noodle, and swim to him. If the current is too strong, at least I'll be attached to the rope."

"A noodle?" Mary Jean asked, clearly confused. "Do you mean an egg noodle? How could that possibly help?"

Despite the circumstances, Lea couldn't help but giggle. "No, I meant to say float. I'll use the log like a float."

Mary Jean gave Lea a disbelieving look, but let it go. "How will you get him back over here?" she asked.

"We can both use the branch and just kick our way back."

Mary Jean nodded.

"I'll be right there!" Lea yelled to the boy.

Mary Jean picked up a long, thick branch and tied the rope swing around its middle in a double knot. Lea held it in front of her and began wading into the creek. She got a few feet out and began swimming toward the boy, the buoyant limb supporting her weight. The wind was blowing and the rain was pouring down. It was hard for Lea to see, and the unusually strong water current pushed her back as she tried to swim forward.

She finally made it to the rock, grasping to it as she caught her breath. She looked at the boy and gasped. He looked just like Sam did when he was younger.

"Sam?" Lea asked.

"My name is Chester," the boy said, trying not to cry. "I'm scared."

Lea was scared too, but Chester wasn't much older than Michael and Emily. Lea knew she had to get him to safety.

"It's okay," Lea said, forcing a smile. We'll get to the creek bank together. Just slide down the rock into the water. I'll help you grab the branch."

Chester sat down on the rock and put his feet into the water. He eased his way into the creek and Lea slid the branch under his stomach. Together, they began kicking their way to land. The wind pushed against them and the rain pelted down in sheets. Amid the chaos, the creek water splashed in their faces, making it difficult to see. Chester almost fell off the log, but Lea grabbed him just in time.

They finally got to Mary Jean, who was kneeling on the bank. She plucked Chester out of the creek, and Lea climbed up beside them, falling onto her stomach as she tried to catch her breath.

"Thank you," Chester said, panting.

"You're welcome. But how did you get to the rock if you can't swim?" Lea asked.

"I waded out to fish earlier this morning, just like every day. It's my job to get fish for dinner, and the water is never much deeper than my knees. I was having trouble catching anything, and then the wind came up and it started to rain. Before I realized it, the water was too deep for me to get back."

"How old are you?" Lea asked.

"Eight," Chester replied.

"Isn't that a little young to be responsible for catching dinner?" Lea asked, thinking about Michael and Emily.

"I live at the orphan farm," said Chester. "We all have chores to do."

Mary Jean and Lea shared a glance, not sure how to reply. Mary Jean changed the subject.

"You should get some dry clothes on. We'll take you back. Where's your fishing pole? Did you lose it when the water started to rise?"

"I use a stick and a line. I'll make another one tomorrow."

The three started walking back to the orphan farm, Chester leading the way. Lea stopped short when she noticed that they were in her future backyard. Mary Jean had figured it out too. But it wasn't Lea's present time, or even 1953. It looked like Lea and Mary Jean had traveled much further back in time.

The farm looked old—it reminded Lea of pictures of farms from the early 1900s that she saw at the school library. It was also in need of a lot of work. The house's paint was faded and chipped, and some of the windows were cracked. An overgrown garden took up most of the backyard, and some poorly dressed children were picking vegetables. A chicken coop, not in much better condition than the house, stood behind the garden.

"Who takes care of you?" Lea asked Chester.

"Miss Philbrick is in charge, but we mostly all take care of each other," he said, pointing to the other children. "My friend Daniel usually comes fishing with me, but he's sick in bed today."

An older woman, her hair in a bun and wearing a long dress covered by an apron, came into the yard. "Did you catch any fish?" she yelled to Chester.

"No," he answered, looking at the ground.

The woman just shook her head and went back inside. She didn't seem to notice that Chester was soaked.

Chester turned to Mary Jean and Lea. "Thanks for saving me. I have to help pick vegetables now."

"Goodbye, Chester," they said together.

As Chester walked to the garden, the wind picked up again and Lea and Mary Jean were soon caught up in a time travel cloud, twisting and turning.

They landed on the road to town, in 1953. Mary Jean's basket of vegetables was on the ground next to them.

As she picked up the basket, Mary Jean said, "I had a feeling you were a time traveler. Especially after you showed up by the fountain in back of the hardware store soaking wet and without shoes on."

"Wait," Lea answered, gasping. "Do you time travel too? Before meeting Chester, I mean."

"Yes," answered Mary Jean. It began when I was thirteen. I traveled back to the early 1900s a few times. This is the first time it's happened in a while, though."

"Do you know why?" Lea could hardly contain her excitement and forced herself to take a deep breath. "Do you know other time travelers? I'm so happy—"

But Mary Jean cut Lea off. "Each time traveler has their own story. You'll learn more, but we shouldn't talk about it now. You're still in the middle of your journey and I don't want to change your course. I'm sure there was a reason for what happened today, and maybe someday we'll know what it is."

Lea wanted to ask more about time travel and Chester, but Mary Jean was done talking. She was about to walk into the church hall with the vegetables, but Lea stopped her.

"Mary Jean, we're soaked."

"I'll just say we got caught in the rain," she answered.

"But what if it didn't rain here? Nothing looks wet."

"Doesn't matter," Mary Jean said. "We still got caught in the rain."

Mary Jean walked into the church hall with the vegetables, but Lea, self-conscious about her appearance, decided to stay outside. Mary Jean returned a few minutes later.

"My mom wants me to stay and help make sandwiches for lunch. Tell Genevieve that I say hi."

Lea left Mary Jean, frustrated that Mary Jean wouldn't talk with her about time traveling, but still excited that she was a time traveler too. And Lea couldn't wait to look at the time capsule stowed in her little hideaway. But first, she had to find Genevieve and give her Harry's ring.

She walked by the hardware store and went down the alley, hoping that Genevieve was sitting near the fountain. Genevieve wasn't there, and Lea felt a pang of regret, but as Lea walked back toward Main Street, she bumped into a girl who was walking out the side door, carrying what appeared to be a large amount of building supplies.

"Genevieve!" Lea said.

Genevieve's face lit up. "Lea! I'm so happy to see you. Will you help me bring this stuff to the apothecary? I don't think I can handle it all on my own in one trip."

Lea took some of the supplies from Genevieve and they started toward the apothecary.

"I'm so embarrassed to be dressed like this," Genevieve said.

Genevieve was wearing her work clothes again—jeans and an old shirt. The water must have finally been cleared out from the apothecary floor because tennis shoes replaced the large rubber boots she had been wearing before.

"You look fine, but now you know how I feel," Lea muttered as she took some items out of Genevieve's arms.

Genevieve stared at Lea for a moment. "Yes, I guess I do. I'm sorry I made such a big deal about your clothes before."

Lea nodded and looked at the ground. She knew that there were times in the present that she judged other people's clothes too—although the circumstances were different, the lesson was the same.

"I'm glad I got to meet you, Lea," Genevieve said as they walked. "It seems like I've known you for a long time even though we only met a few days ago. I hope we'll always be friends."

"Me too," answered Lea. "There's something familiar about you, but I don't know what it is. It's like we've met before."

Genevieve laughed. "We sound like two old ladies. I guess it's just the storm making us grateful for what we have."

Lea laughed too. "I guess so!"

They were almost at the apothecary. A few men on the roof worked, making the repairs that Mary Jean had told

Lea about. Looking closer, Lea could see that Harold was up there too. He grinned and waved at Genevieve.

"I feel so bad for Harold's family," Genevieve murmured. "They won't be able to open the store again for at least another two weeks. The roof needs to be redone, and the water that came in through the hole in the roof damaged most of the merchandise. Even the soda fountain was destroyed."

The girls were close enough to hear the men talking. "Harry, Harry Perkins?" came a panicked voice from the roof. "Harold, for Pete's sake, pay attention to what you're doing!"

The girls looked up in time to see Harold almost fall off the roof. Genevieve gasped, and then sighed as he regained his balance at the last second.

The man who had been yelling at Harry looked to see what he was staring at and began to laugh. "Oh, now I understand. Genny's here. Go ahead, son, climb down and see your girl. Just watch your step."

Genevieve blushed and Lea smiled. Harry climbed down the ladder from the roof as the girls got to the apothecary.

"Hi Genevieve," Harry said as he took the building supplies from her and set them down next to the ladder. He didn't acknowledge Lea, so she put hers on the ground too. Genevieve and Harold were looking all goofy at each other again, so Lea decided to walk around the back of the store and pretend she was interested in the roof repairs. It wouldn't be long before Harold was back on the roof and she could hand his ring off to Genevieve.

But as Lea was walking, looking up at the roof, she tripped on a branch and stumbled forward.

The ground rushed up to meet her face—and opened into the now-familiar tunnel. Lea found herself back in the darkness, twisting and turning, until she landed back in the present, right next to the rope swing near the creek.

As she looked around, stunned to be back, Lea felt Harold's ring pressing into her leg.

"*Ugh!*" she shouted, and she stamped her foot so hard that she lost her balance and almost fell into the creek. She had been given the perfect opportunity to give Harold's ring back to Genevieve, and she hadn't taken it. Why had she been transported back to the present so quickly? She was so frustrated that she wanted to cry. Lea wiped a tear off her cheek, promising herself that no matter what, the next time she got back to 1953, she would get the ring to Genevieve before she did anything else.

Dejected, Lea walked slowly toward the house, upset that she had let such a great opportunity pass her by. Then she remembered the time capsule. Her spirits picking up, Lea ran toward the house, hoping that the time capsule would still be in the wall in her special place at the back of her closet.

Lea yelled a quick "Hello" to no one in particular as she burst into the house, half-walking, half-jogging toward the stairs. She bounded up them, two at a time, and ran down the hall into her bedroom, closing the door behind her. She went to the back of her closet and into the back room under the eaves when she heard a loud knock on her bedroom door, followed by Mom's stressed out voice saying, "Lea, come downstairs. We're having an unexpected lunch guest and I need your help getting ready."

Lea opened her bedroom door in a huff. "Right now? I was just about to do something important."

"Sorry, honey. It's going to have to wait. A friend of Gramma's is back in town for a wedding, and today is the only time she has to see her. They haven't seen each other since Grampa Perkins died. Sam is vacuuming, and I have to run to the store to get some extra things for lunch. I need you to make a fruit salad and set the table."

Lea sighed, frustrated at her lack of progress with the class ring and now with the time capsule, and closed her bedroom door forcefully and walked downstairs behind her mother.

CHAPTER TEN

Downstairs, Michael and Emily were playing Crazy 8s in the family room and Gramma was sleeping in her chair. Lea hoped that Gramma's nap would improve her mood.

As instructed, Lea made a fruit salad. Just as she finished setting the table, Mom walked in with the groceries. As Lea helped put them away, she noticed that Mom had bought bologna. If the nap didn't help with Gramma's mood, the bologna definitely would.

Mom went into Gramma's room to wake her up and help her get ready for company. Lea wandered around the downstairs, picking up and wondering what Gramma's friend would be like. Gramma wasn't all that old—she was eighty-one. Lots of eighty-one-year-olds live alone, drove cars, and have fun with their family and friends. But Alzheimer's disease made her seem like a very old lady, and Gramma couldn't do any of that.

Then Lea smiled when she remembered Gramma hula hooping, riding Starburst, and enjoying the play in the park. When she was given the chance, Gramma could still have fun, even with Alzheimer's.

The chime of the doorbell interrupted Lea's thoughts.

"Lea, I'm still helping Gramma get ready. Please get the door," Mom shouted from Gramma's room.

Lea opened the door to a pleasant-looking woman with chin-length brown hair and pretty caramel-brown eyes. Lea stared, dumbstruck. *Could this be Mary Jean?* Looking at her distinctly colored eyes, Lea knew it had to be. Lea had just seen Mary Jean an hour ago, but at that time, Mary Jean was sixteen. The Mary Jean standing at the door was eighty-one. Although Lea recognized Mary Jean, Mary Jean didn't seem to remember Lea.

"You must be Lea," Mary Jean said, extending her hand.

Lea mechanically shook Mary Jean's hand, still staring. Thankfully, Gramma must have heard Mary Jean's greeting to Lea, because she rushed into the kitchen, practically pushing Lea down to get to her friend. The two women embraced, both with tears in their eyes.

Lea would never understand how Gramma could remember some people and things and not others. The past was clear, but the present was a mystery. For about the thousandth time, Lea wondered what Gramma was like before Alzheimer's.

Mom ushered everyone into the family room and brought in lemonade and iced tea. Sam joined the twins in their game of Crazy 8s, but Lea wanted to hear the conversation between Gramma and Mary Jean.

At first the conversation was awkward. Even though Gramma remembered Mary Jean, she was still confused, the effects of Alzheimer's obvious. Mary Jean and Mom talked about all the things going on in Cabot Corner, and Mary Jean spoke with Lea and her siblings, asking how old everyone was and what grade each would be in when school started in a couple of weeks. It wasn't until the conversation turned to last week's storm that things got interesting.

"Did you hear about the storm we had last week?" Mom asked Mary Jean. "We were lucky not to have any damage on the farm other than a few downed trees, but the creek flooded and a few people in town lost their roofs."

"I did hear it was quite a storm," Mary Jean answered.

And then Mary Jean spoke to Gramma.

"Genny, do you remember the big storm back in 1953 when the apothecary was damaged?"

Gramma nodded. "That was a terrible storm. We lost power, and while it was out, I lost Harry's ring in the darkness. I was so upset. And then the roof of the apothecary caved in. Harry's family didn't have insurance, and they almost lost everything. But the whole town came together to help them save their business."

Everything around Lea had gone blank. It was like she was sitting alone in an empty room bathed in white light where she couldn't hear or feel anything.

Genevieve is Gramma. Genevieve is Gramma. Genevieve is Gramma.

The words played over and over in Lea's mind, getting louder with each repetition until they were screaming in her head like clashing cymbals. It was an impossible thought, but deep inside, Lea knew it was true. As she began to understand what had happened over the past several days, her senses returned, and Lea could again hear the conversation between Gramma and Mary Jean.

"Do you remember when we put on the plays in the park each summer, Genny?" Mary Jean asked.

"Yes. I loved writing and performing. We were very popular because of those plays," Gramma added.

The two women continued to reminisce about their childhoods in Cabot Corner. Mary Jean would prompt Gramma with a question about something they had done together, and Gramma would talk about it as best as she could. They spoke about swimming in the creek, getting sodas at the apothecary, and riding Star.

Lea sat in awe as she listened to Gramma and Mary

Jean. She thought back to last week's storm and remembered Gramma crying when the power went out and saying, "I couldn't find it." She must have thought she was back in 1953 when she lost Harry's ring.

That's it, Lea realized. The time travel magic had been giving her hints each time she traveled back to 1953. Lea thought back to the wish she made on Sunday after Gramma had been lost. She wanted to be closer to Gramma, and during this week that had started to happen. Best of all, Lea had been given the chance to know Gramma before she had Alzheimer's, something she had wanted.

Mom had gone into the kitchen to get lunch ready, and Sam and the twins had lost interest in their card game and were outside on the swing set. Gramma was talking to Mary Jean about the past, but Mary Jean stared at Lea. As Lea met her gaze, Mary Jean smiled and subtly nodded, as if she knew what Lea had just discovered.

Mom called everyone to the kitchen for lunch where Gramma, Mary Jean, and Lea enjoyed bologna on white bread and everyone else had turkey on whole grain.

"Did you know that I used to live in this house?" Mary Jean asked Sam and the twins as she finished up some fruit salad.

Lea just kept her eyes down, fixated on her remaining potato chips, but Sam and the twins were very excited to hear this.

"When?" asked Sam.

"Where did you sleep?" asked Emily.

"Does it look the same?" asked Michael.

Mary Jean laughed. "I lived here until I got married in 1957. My bedroom was the one with the windows that looks out over the pasture, and some things are the same, but a lot has changed. It was a long time ago. But there are a lot of special places in this house, and even some secret places and things." And then Mary Jean looked directly at Lea.

The twins gasped in delight at the thought of secret places in their house, and Lea looked up to meet Mary Jean's gaze. This time it was Lea who nodded, conveying to Mary Jean that she remembered what she had told her about the time capsule.

The lunch conversation had been fun and lively, but it was a lot for Gramma. She fell asleep at the table, exhausted from the visit.

"Thank you for a lovely visit and lunch," Mary Jean said to all of them. "It has been such a treat to see Genny and get to know her grandchildren."

Mom hugged Mary Jean and helped Gramma to her room for a nap. Lea walked Mary Jean to her car.

"I'm glad that I got to see you in present time, Mary Jean," Lea said, thinking it was strange to be calling an eighty-one-year-old woman by her first name and thinking of her as a friend. "But it was extra special to know you as a teenager—Gramma too. I understand so much more about her than I did."

"Time travel is a gift," Mary Jean answered. "But you know that now."

"How does the magic know who to pick?" Lea asked.

"The magic lives in the farmhouse and it chooses the people living there who need it the most."

Lea waved as Mary Jean backed out of the driveway. Before Mary Jean turned onto the street toward town, she put her window down and spoke to Lea once more. "Don't forget about the time capsule. It's your responsibility to keep the magic going."

Lea nodded and watched Mary Jean drive out of sight.

As Lea walked back into the house, she felt Harold's high school ring dig into her leg. Lea smiled as she realized that it belonged to her grandfather.

Lea went back to her room, anxious to look for the time capsule. She closed the door to her room and then the door to her closet. From the back of her closet she grabbed her beanbag chair and shoved it against her closet door. Running her fingers over the drywall, Lea found the cut and gently pulled it out. She reached into the hole, finding a shoebox resting against the joists in the eaves. Lea pulled out the box and placed it on the floor. She carefully pulled off the lid and removed a sheet of tissue paper that covered the contents.

The box held pictures of Mary Jean and her family, the farm, and newspaper clippings about a family wedding and a few civic events. There was even an article about Mary Jean's horse, Star, being born. At the very bottom of the box, though, was a sealed manila envelope. Lea carefully split apart the top of the envelope and pulled out a newspaper clipping that was attached to a note. The newspaper clipping was from 1885! It was a story about two unnamed girls who had rescued a boy from a rock in the creek during a sudden violent rainstorm. The boy's name was Chester Clark. The note attached to the clipping stated:

If you're reading this, you have also experienced the magic of time travel. Before you move out of this house, leave some artifacts about your family in this box, along with something you have from the year to which you traveled. The time travel magic will take care of the rest.

A loud knock on her bedroom door jolted Lea back to reality. The she heard Mom's voice. "Lea, open the door! I've been calling to you for five minutes."

Lea quickly put the box into the eaves and placed the sheetrock back in its place. She ran into the main part of her room and opened the door.

"What are you doing?" Mom asked.

"I was just reading in the back of the closet."

"Well, bring your book downstairs with Gramma for a little bit. Sam is outside with Jeremy and I'm taking the twins shopping for new sneakers."

Gramma was still sleeping when Lea first walked into her room, but after Mom and the twins left, she opened her eyes. Lea realized that Gramma must have been crying in her sleep. There were tears in her eyes and her cheeks were wet.

"What's wrong, Gramma?" Lea asked.

"I miss my Harry," Gramma said. "I wish I could see him like I got to see Mary Jean."

Lea finally realized why the time travel magic hadn't allowed her to give Harold's ring back to Genevieve in 1953.

"Gramma, I got to see Grampa Harry a few times this week, and I know that he loves you very much. Best of all, I found something that you lost a long time ago."

Lea pulled her grandfather's class ring out of her pocket and put it in Gramma's hand. Gramma looked at it in disbelief. She started crying again, but this time, they were tears of joy. The ring was still on the same chain that Genevieve had placed it on years ago. Gramma put it around her neck, and took hold of Lea's hand.

"Thank you, Lea. I don't how you found this, but I'm so happy. You're a good granddaughter."

And then Gramma did something she had never done before. She picked up her candy dish and offered it to Lea.

"Would you like a piece of chocolate?" she asked.

Lea smiled and took a piece.

After I gave Grampa's class ring back to Gramma, the time travel magic disappeared, and my life returned to normal. I resumed hiking and swimming with my friends and riding Starburst. School started a couple of weeks later, and I was soon busy with homework and sports. My relationship with Gramma stayed strong. We even got to ride together a few times before Alzheimer's—and old age in general—made it too difficult for Gramma to get on Starburst. We continued to go to plays and movies and look at old photo albums together, and Gramma continued to share her chocolate with me.

The summer before my senior year in high school, I had the chance to travel back in time once more. I was walking alone by the creek on a beautiful Saturday morning when the rope swing beckoned to me. At first, I didn't recognize what was happening. But after a couple times of it swinging back and forth right in front of me, I caught on. I grabbed the rope and held it tight. I twisted and turned through time, finally landing on the sidewalk in front of the Baptist church in Cabot Corner, 1957. In front of me stood Genevieve, radiant in a white wedding gown, holding the arm of an older man who looked like Uncle Carlton. Genevieve was happy to see me, and didn't mention my clothes, even though I was in my favorite attire of shorts and a tank top.

"Lea, I was hoping you would show up today! Harold and I are getting married," she told me. Then Genevieve looked at the man standing next to her. "This is my father, Mr. Chester Clark. Daddy, this is my friend, Lea."

I smiled at my great grandfather, who said, "Yes, I think we've met before. You must attend the wedding."

Although I was terribly self-conscious about my clothing, I took a seat in the back, not willing to give up the honor of watching my grandparents exchange wedding vows just because of my appearance. The ceremony was beautiful, and I was surprised that even after all the time that had passed, Genevieve and Harold were still all goofy when they looked at each other.

I had hoped to congratulate them, but walking out of the church, I tripped, and for the last time, traveled through the dark tunnel, back to the present.

Gramma passed away on the farm the summer before I left for college on the East Coast. She had given Grampa Harry's class ring to me in a rare moment of mental clarity just a few weeks before she died. The ring meant a great deal to me, but in my heart, I knew it didn't truly belong to me. The ring belonged to the time travel magic. Just as it had brought Gramma and me together, perhaps it would one day do the same for others.

The day before I left for my new home, a dorm room in New Hampshire, I once again closed the door to my bedroom and placed my now worn beanbag chair in front of the closet door. Although I had been adding pictures and newspaper clippings to the time capsule since I had discovered it, I still had one task left to accomplish. With shaking hands, I gently removed the cut piece of sheetrock from the wall and found the time capsule in the eaves. I took out the worn old box and removed the cover, and then, the thinning tissue paper that covered the box's contents. Taking a long last look at my grandfather's high school ring, something that had been so important to both my grandmother and me, and to the relationship we eventually shared, I placed it with a note in a plastic bag, and added it to the shoebox. The note read:

This ring belonged to my grandfather, Harold Perkins. He gave it to his girlfriend and future wife, Genevieve Clark in 1953, but it was lost until the time travel magic found it. If you're reading this note, you already know how clever the time travel magic is, and how it uses ordinary objects to change lives. Please leave pictures of your family and objects from the years in which you live in this house with the time capsule. Most importantly, before you move out of this special home, please leave an artifact from the year to which you traveled. The time travel magic will take care of the rest.

I often think about who the next time traveler will be and when or if I will meet this person on their journey. I trust the time travel magic though, and I believe that when the time is right, it will all come together. In the meantime, I will continue to look for the magic around me and bask in the wonder of the inexplicable.

ABOUT THE AUTHOR

Kelly McIntire is a marketing professional, turned stay-at-home mom, turned children's author who believes that magic and adventure should begin in childhood and last a lifetime. *Time Twisted* is her debut novel.

Made in the USA
Lexington, KY
13 March 2019